Last Night in Managua

Last Night in Managua
a novel

by James Pendleton

Brandylane Publishers, Inc.

ISBN: 978-1-883911-90-4

Library of Congress Control Number: 2009942952

Brandylane Publishers, Inc.
Richmond, Virginia
www.brandylanepublishers.com

To Lynda, without whose help this manuscript could never have been assembled.

Acknowledgements

Lelia Pendleton, Boyd Grandstaff, Vladimir Bubulac,
for their help in manuscript preparation.

Nanette de Garcia, Head of the Group for Mutual Aid
of Guatemala, for her courage and inspiration,

Tomás Borgé, former Minister of the Interior,
Republic of Nicaragua,

Ernesto Cardenál, poet and former Minister of Culture,
Republic of Nicaragua.

1

For weeks afterward, it was there at the most unexpected moments. Whether he was driving his car or pouring coffee or talking to Shufford or Brad or Liliana, the picture of the burning airplane would suddenly burst behind his eyes, sometimes far away, with the fireball orange and black, and sometimes close-up—but always erasing everything else in sight—and Hartley would be thinking of Billy dead at the end of the runway and feeling that somehow he was partly responsible.

Hartley had watched the whole thing happen. He'd seen the line boy drive the jet fuel truck toward the airplane on the field before Billy took off, but he'd paid absolutely no attention until Billy was already roaring down the runway and the line boy was parking the truck back beside the chain link fence.

"What fuel did you put in that airplane?" Hartley had yelled at the line boy, then. But the boy hadn't heard him over the engine noise, and Hartley had jumped up on the running board to yell into the open window, "Junius, what fuel...?" And that was where his memory always moved into fast forward—Junius pointing at the yellow "Av-Jet" sign on the side of the truck and Hartley himself jumping away and running toward the office, pushing through the swinging door and snatching the Unicom mike away from the clerk all in one motion. "Beechcraft four-six-zero, this is Agecroft. Beechcraft four-six-zero, Billy, can you hear me?"

He could see the plane through the plate glass window, already 200 feet above the runway. "Beechcraft four-six-zero...." And then he heard Billy's Alabama flavored voice crackling above the engines, "Roger, partner. What's the problem?"

"Billy, Junius put jet fuel in your gas tanks! Your engine's gonna quit when it mixes."

"Jet fuel!? Jesus!" In all of their time flying together—in combat, through ground fire and God knew what else—it was the first time he'd ever heard Billy even slightly rattled about anything. "O.K., O.K. I'm comin' in."

"Be careful," Hartley said. "Be real careful." And then, as he watched the plane begin its turn back to the runway, he pressed the transmit button once again. "Mayday, Mayday! Attention, all aircraft near Agecroft Field. We have a crippled airplane approaching for landing. Stay clear." And that had been all he could do. If he'd still been in the army, he would have called the fire truck and ambulance crew. But there was no fire truck or ambulance within five miles of Agecroft.

"What's gonna happen, Ron?" the clerk said. "What...?"

But Hartley was already outside on the tarp looking up as the Beechcraft continued its turn toward the runway, the engines missing now, backfiring, pop, pop, and roaring out of sync. "Oh, Jesus," he whispered. "Jesus save him!" And then he just watched as the plane came on across the trees, left wing low, banking into the final turn. And he was whispering, "If only that lower engine doesn't quit now..." when it quit.

Billy couldn't get the wing up. He was only a hundred feet above ground, still short of the runway, and just as the engine on the low wing quit, the opposite engine surged with a sudden burst of life, and the plane gave a half roll and went down inverted to explode like a bomb in a ball of orange flame and black smoke, and Hartley knew that even if the ambulance medics had been there, they would have had nothing to do.

Bob Shufford nearly beat the line boy to death. Shufford had been on the telephone in the back office when he heard Hartley's Mayday call. And he'd run behind Hartley to the crash site where they both had to stop helpless in the heat as the metal of the wings turned red. "Why?" Shufford said. "Why did it happen?"

"Because Junius put jet fuel in the gas tank," Hartley said. And Shufford went crazy. Junius had followed them to the wreckage, and Shufford turned and flattened him on the taxiway with one blow. "You son of a bitch!" Hartley could see the blood and the vacancies in the kid's mouth where his front teeth had been, and then Shufford was on top of him, still slugging him on the ground and screaming, "You worthless bastard! You have just killed one of the best pilots! You have just destroyed one of the finest airplanes!"

And Hartley was trying to pull Shufford away. "Come on Bob. Leave him alone."

"Let go of me!" Shufford said.

"It's not his fault."

"Get your hands off me!"

Shufford slugged the boy again, peeling back the skin on the kid's cheek as Hartley grabbed him under the arms and pulled from behind so the boy could get up. "If I ever see you again, I'll kill you!" Shufford was shouting. And his boot flashed forward making full contact with the boy's ass, flattening him as he tried to rise. "I'll kill you!" he shouted again, now jerking away from Hartley and turning, "Take your hands off me! What d'ya mean, 'not his fault'?"

"It's the pilot's responsibility, like it says in the regulations."

"Shit, Ron! You can't live in aviation if somebody fucks up! We're ruined! Do you understand that?"

"What?"

"It's all over. The goddamned business. It's finished."

"What're you talkin' about?"

And then Shufford stopped suddenly and looked into Hartley's eyes. "Ron, who's gonna tell his wife?"

2

Of course, it was Hartley who told her. "Unless *you* want to tell her," he'd said to Shufford, "since you're the boss of this outfit."

"No, you go ahead. You speak her damn language."

"Hell! She speaks English as well as anybody...."

"When a woman gets a shock, she reverts," Shufford said. "She'll start talkin' her own language—Spanish—whatever it is. She needs somebody who can handle it. Besides, you know her better."

And that's when the flashbacks started. No sooner had Hartley parked his stained old Austin-Healey in front of Billy's house than he was suddenly back at the airport reliving every minute of the afternoon, from the moment he'd first seen the fuel truck on the field to the moment of the fireball. God!

He turned off the engine but just sat there in his car without moving, seeing it all, the plane banking in across the trees and then the roll, but seeing it now in slow motion from inside the cockpit just as Billy must have seen it when the plane inverted and started down....

If only he had noticed sooner, he thought, if only he'd said something to Junius sooner! Jesus!

His arms and shoulders were trembling, and Hartley knew he couldn't speak to anybody right then, so he started the car again and drove around the block to the edge of a nearby lake where he got out and just stood looking at the water. For a long time, the fireball wouldn't go away. But, finally, it was all right, and he drove back to park again over the damp leaves in front of Billy's house, taking a deep breath and dreading now the words he would have to speak.

But Liliana Summerfield knew the whole story before Hartley said anything at all. He'd never been to the house without Billy, and he'd never been there at all in the afternoon, and she had the full picture the moment she saw him. Coming to the lattice door in a white dress that made her Spanish and Indian heritage even more obvious than usual, she simply said, "No.... No.... God, no!" and pulled away from him into the darkened house.

Hartley just waited until she turned back, and then, as the tears came, she leaned heavily against his arm and allowed him to conduct her to the sofa as he gave her the details.

"What can I do?" Hartley said. She continued sitting like a statue while he made coffee in the kitchen and brought her a cup. "What can I do? Is there anyone I can call? Relatives? Friends? Insurance companies...?" He heard a car, and through the window he could see Shufford and his wife Maude approaching the house. "We want to do everything we can to help," he said.

3

It was not until after Billy's funeral that Hartley found out it really was all over. He'd ignored Shufford's comment after the accident, but he began to get the full picture three days later as they drove away from the funeral service in Shufford's black Buick. "Did Liliana say anything about going back to her own country?" Shufford said.

"No. Why?"

"What's the name of it?"

"Nicaragua."

"I never can remember the names of those little banana republics. Is that the same place you lived when you were a kid?"

"Yes." Hartley was in the back seat and he could see Shufford's eyes in the rear view mirror.

"Well, if you get a chance, recommend it," Shufford said.

"Recommend what?" Shufford's wife said.

"Going back, Maude. Going back. I'd feel a hell of a lot better if she was safe in another country before she got the idea of smackin' us with a lawsuit of some kind."

And suddenly, for no clear reason, Hartley's pulse was racing in alarm. "Why would she do that?" he said.

But Shufford seemed not to hear the question as he spoke to his wife and pointed toward their office beyond the entrance to the airport. "Er..., Maude, we'll just get off here, and Ron can drive me home after we talk about some things."

The clerk was gone, and there was only one student pilot shooting landings in a Cessna 150 as they walked into the silent building.

"You want coffee?" Shufford said.

"No. I'm on my way to meet my family in Richmond."

"It was good to see your brother at the funeral."

"Yeah, I was surprised," Hartley said.

Normally Shufford would have sat down and put his feet on the desk, but today he just led the way into his office and stood at the window looking out at the Cessna as it circled for another approach. "We're gonna miss Billy," he said.

"Yeah," Hartley said. "A lot. Fuel contamination of all things! He was always so careful."

"Everybody will fuck up sometime."

"Hmm, maybe."

"No *maybe* about it. You can bet on it." Shufford looked at the scarred knuckles of his right hand. "We're all gonna fuck up big sometime. It may not always be fatal, but the big one is out there someplace waiting for us."

"What are you talking about, Bob?"

Shufford turned from the window and squinted at Hartley. "I forgot to send in the insurance payment on time."

"You what?!"

"It lapsed the week before Billy's accident."

Hartley just frowned and looked at him in the darkening office, for a moment speechless as a sudden wave of heat rose around his ears the way it had done once when his engine had quit at six thousand feet.

"What I'm tellin' you is, we're finished," Shufford said. "The company, jobs, everything."

"How in hell could you forget the insurance?"

"We were low on cash, so I decided to wait out the grace period...."

"Jesus!"

"...Then I forgot."

"I owned half that airplane! That's half my house!"

"It would've been touch and go even without the crash," Shufford said. "But now, with the recession and high interest rates and business all but dead...."

"Stupid," Hartley said.

"...We've got debts so far up the ass I can taste 'em."

"Totally stupid!" Hartley was shouting now, "I put everything I had into this company!" leaning across the desk, "Totally, totally stupid!" And suddenly he wanted to leap the desk and pound Shufford's face against the floor the way Shufford had pounded Junius, but instead, he just turned and walked out, pushing through the swinging gate in the outer office and not even bothering to look back at the sound of Shufford's voice.

4

"So now what?" Brad said. They were in the den after dinner, and Hartley was standing at the French doors looking out at the fountain in the rose garden. "What're you going to do?"

He had driven directly to his brother's house, fled really, at eighty miles an hour up the interstate, through the Virginia countryside, toward Richmond, to the heart of his family, wanting to see them, yet remembering now a strange sense of embarrassment as he had pulled into the circular drive before the big house on Loch Lane and staggered up the steps to find Brad in the front hall. "Give me a drink," he'd said, and Brad had led him to the kitchen where his sister-in-law made noises of concern as he downed two old-fashioneds in quick succession.

"Be careful. You know how Mother is about drinking."

"I'll try to remember," Hartley had said. And then, gulping the second one, he had heard his mother calling him from the stairs, "Ronnie! Where are you?"

If she noticed the whiskey on his breath, she never mentioned it. Coming down the winding stairs, tall and stately as ever, she embraced him in front of the dining room door, surrounding him with the familiar scent of lavender as she looked into his eyes. "It's so good to be having dinner with *both* of my sons for a change. Ronnie, we miss you!"

"I know, Mother. I miss you, too."

She was suddenly frowning. "Your color's not good. Are you eating right?"

"Yes, of course, I learned nutrition at my mother's knee."

"Well, good. I'm delighted to hear it. At least you're not neglecting yourself. Now if you'd stop neglecting your family so terribly, everything would be all right."

Once again, he had failed to measure up. "I'm sorry," he said. "I've been doing a lot of flying lately, and with this accident...."

"Oh, I know it must have been horrible. Ronnie, when are you going to give up this dangerous flying business and come back among your own people where you belong?"

It was a question she had been asking since Vietnam, and he'd always hedged on it, half joking, "Maybe one day," or "Just as soon as I get rich." But tonight, even though he wanted to avoid talking about events at the airport, he didn't want to hedge on anything at all. "Who knows?" he said. "The way things are going, it may be sooner than we think."

"I get the feeling that the future of Swift Aviation is less than rosy," Brad said at his back.

And suddenly Hartley couldn't help himself. "All right!" he said. "All right." In spite of all his plans not to talk about it, he stopped beside the dining room table and turned to face them, hearing the anger in his voice as he spoke. "Let's get this out in the open once and for all: The future of Swift Aviation is *nonexistent*, totally nonexistent. The company's finished, the planes are for sale to the highest bidder, and your favorite prodigal is out of work. If you have any more questions, I hope you'll save them till after dinner."

And then he'd apologized. "I'm sorry," he said. "It's been a hard week."

"What're you going to do?" Brad said, and this time Hartley turned from the French doors and walked back toward his chair beside the brandy on the coffee table.

"Who knows? We're bankrupt."

"On a single loss?"

He told Brad about Shufford and the insurance. "But besides that, there's no new business," he said. "And with interest rates running at twenty percent, it's impossible...."

"So how are you fixed?"

"You want me to grovel on the floor?"

"No, not at all," Brad said.

"You were right and I was wrong. You gave me good advice and I ignored you. It was a lousy time to start a business."

Brad dismissed it with a wave of his hand. "So tell me how you're fixed."

"Aside from losing my investment, my job, and a good friend, I'm fine."

"I'm sorry."

"And since I'd already lost my wife and helped lose a war in Southeast Asia, I suppose you could say your little brother is among the world's all-time losers."

"Diana called yesterday, by the way, speaking of your wife—or your ex-wife."

"Great." Hartley ran his open hand across his chest. "Let me see if I've got any more wounds I can open."

"Ronnie, she was being nice. She said she was sorry about Billy."

"Thanks for the message."

"I didn't realize it would upset you."

"Yeah, well, these are upsetting times."

Brad picked up the brandy bottle from the coffee table and poured two glasses. "I've got a place for you, if you want it."

"What do you mean, you've got a place for me?"

"At the bank."

"Brad, come on. Be serious. I can hear you now trying to convince your board."

"No, wait.... Let me tell you."

"The all-time loser—I'd be an embarrassment and you know it."

"No. When you worked at the bank before, you did a perfectly fine job."

"I quit on you. Why would you risk me again?"

"Ronnie, listen. I understand perfectly why you didn't like the bank before. After running fire missions and pulling wounded off the field in Vietnam, you had to be bored to death at the bank."

"So why am I better now?"

"You've got the kind of experience we need."

"Doing what?"

"Checking on foreign investments."

"I don't have experience in foreign investments."

"No, and not many of us do. But you do have experience in banking, and you do have experience in the Third World. You'd get to use your Spanish again."

"Where?"

"Central America, South America."

"Traveling?"

Brad nodded. "Maybe even go back to Nicaragua. Everybody down there wants to enter the industrial age, compete on world markets. And God knows they need financing."

"It's been a long time...."

"So what? We need somebody who knows how to get along down there, somebody who knows the language, knows the culture. I thought about it today at the funeral when I saw you talking to Billy's widow."

"...A long time," Hartley said again, "both for the banking and the Spanish."

"Ronnie, listen, this is a brand new thing. You can brush up. If it's the sort of thing that interests you—I tell you, there's money to be made."

"You won't call me 'Ronnie' if I work at the bank, will you?"

"You don't like it?"

"I hate it."

Brad laughed and pushed the brandy snifter forward across the table. "You going to try this?"

5

Since he had no appointment, he had to wait for nearly an hour in the soundproof reception room outside Brad's office. But when Brad finally came out to meet him, he threw such an enthusiastic arm around Hartley's shoulder that he forgot the delay altogether. "Ron, come in," Brad said. "I'm sorry you had to wait."

"It's all right," Hartley said. "I should have called."

"I was afraid you were going to turn me down on this thing."

"No," Hartley said. "Not yet anyway. I want to learn more."

"O.K. Great! Come on." And Brad led the way back, beyond the brass sign that read, "Bradford Hartley, Vice President," to his private suite, pausing only to introduce Hartley to his new secretary as they passed her desk.

"So give me some details about this job."

Brad continued to his own desk, then turned without sitting and leaned thoughtfully back against the front edge as he looked at Hartley in the easy chair. "I suppose," he said, "the question before us is, 'How does a bank make money in times of high interest, high inflation, and a depressed market?'"

"With great difficulty," Hartley said.

Brad laughed. "Yes. With very great difficulty. But it can be done. And one answer is to go outside the country." He moved toward his own chair and then suddenly turned back toward the door. "But, hell, why sit here to tell you? I can show you a lot better."

"Outside the country?"

"Come on. You'll see." He motioned for Hartley to follow as he told Miss Carter where they were going, and five minutes later, they were driving out of the parking lot in Brad's black Mercedes. "We have a client—the Ajax Feed and Equipment Company—who owes us over a million dollars," Brad said. "I'm going to show you." They crossed the James River Bridge and moved into the industrial part of south Richmond, past tobacco warehouses and the pine and creosote smell of builders' supplies and lumber yards. And then, as Brad turned the corner onto the narrow end of Hull Street, he pointed to a large compound of brightly painted farm equipment—tractors, harvesters, disks, rakes, harrows, irrigation equipment—enclosed behind a six-foot chain link fence. "The Ajax Company," he said, "largest distributor of farm equipment in the Southeast." He stopped and turned off the ignition. "The problem is, they can't pay. They owe us a million dollars—more. And they can't even meet their interest payments."

"Are you going to foreclose?"

"The bank is not in the tractor business."

"But you are," Hartley said. "Or you soon will be, whether you like it or not."

Brad looked at him as he opened the car door. "My job—and your job, if you take it—is to find ways to make sure we're not."

They walked along beside the dirt street then, through the dust sprinkled weeds that lined the ditch and on around the full circumference of the yard. "You see, this guy—and that's his name, by the way, Walter Guy—this guy at Ajax can't pay us because his customers, the farmers, can't pay him until they can raise a decent crop and get good prices for their produce. But God—or somebody—has been extremely unkind to farmers lately. Low prices, high interest, and drought for three years running."

"It's a pretty grim picture."

"Grim, hell! It's a damn disaster!" Brad waved his arm over the compound. "Most of this stuff has already been repossessed at least once by the dealer. And there it sits: expensive, complex, almost magical equipment that right now is not worth the cost of a shoe shine on the U.S. market."

"So what's the answer?" Hartley said.

"To make Ajax Equipment profitable."

"Is that really the bank's job?"

"Hell yes! When somebody owes you a million dollars, yes. And that's where you come in."

"I thought you wanted me to do something with foreign investments."

"I do. And this is it. Ajax has a customer. Maybe a big customer. And guess where he is."

"I don't know."

"Right in our old home town of Managua, Nicaragua, Central America."

"You're kidding."

Brad nodded toward the Mercedes. "Let's go back to the office, and I'll explain it."

When they reached the seventeenth floor of First International Bank, Hartley stood for a long moment beside the glass wall that provided the pictorial setting for Brad's desk. He could see the streets below and the parks and the turnpikes filled with tiny cars, and on across the rocks of the river, he could see the industrial areas they had just visited. "You're like God up here, aren't you?" he said as Brad came back from the washroom.

"Who?"

"You—looking down on all the little people who need money."

Brad laughed and laid a folder marked "Ajax" across the end of the mahogany conference table that occupied the right side of his office. "Don't let appearances fool you," he said. "Those little people can make us or break us." He opened the folder and motioned for Hartley to join him. "Let me show you the story on Ajax." He flipped through the stack of letters, bills, contracts, and extensions until he came to the final tally sheet. "It's really very simple," he said. "They owe us one million, two hundred thousand dollars and can't pay. But now suddenly they have this potential customer in the form of a large agricultural consortium known as 'Agri-21' whose offices are in the city of Managua, Nicaragua. Agri-21 wants to buy farm equipment, especially good, used equipment—which

Walter Guy has plenty of at Ajax. But Agri-21 also needs financing. So last week, Walter Guy came to me and pointed out that, if we could finance his customer, he could pay us what he owes and we would once again have our money productively invested."

"Which sounds like a fine idea," Hartley said.

"If Agri-21 can pay its debts," Brad said. He looked directly into his brother's eyes. "And that, Ronald, will be your job, if you come with the bank: Go see these guys, get to know them.... Find out whether or not we ought to invest in this company and then help us get a line on other opportunities in the area."

"Be a financial ambassador, huh?"

"Exactly. And I might add also that the U.S. government encourages banks to make such loans whenever possible—to help these little countries stay afloat."

Hartley sighed and looked out of the window.

"What's the matter?"

"I was just thinking about the U.S. farmers who'll lose their tractors."

"Don't get sentimental."

"Don't worry. I gave up sentimentality when I came out of Cambodia."

"Like hell you did."

"I understand there's a lot of political unrest down there."

"Hell, Ronnie, there's always political unrest in Latin America— like soccer and bananas. Some macho general decides to make himself president. But it never bothers business much because, no matter who gets into office, they've still got to deal with Uncle Sam."

"Hmm."

"Unless it goes like Cuba and the reds get in," Brad said. "But of course, there's nothing like thriving business to keep the reds out." Brad looked away, and this time when he looked back, his smile was gone. "Are you going to take this job or not?"

6

He thought about it now as he settled into the seat of the 727 bound for Miami. There had been enough talk, enough shuffling, and Brad, in his typical way, had focused everything with his one brusque question: "Are you going to take this job or not?" And Hartley had said, "Hell, yes! I never felt so much like a banker in all my life. Yes, I'm going to take it!"

He had met with the bank president and a couple of vice presidents who had all signed off on rehiring him. And now, in what seemed to be a very short time, he was seated on an Eastern Airline flight to Miami where he was scheduled to change to Aeronica for the flight to Nicaragua. He looked out the window as the big plane moved onto the runway, and there was just an instant of sadness as he felt the thrust of the engines pushing him into the seat. His feet automatically pressed against the floor where the rudder pedals would be, and he realized that he had flown his last commercial flight. *Sic transit Gloria*, he thought. Then he sat back to enjoy the ride.

Most of the flight was above the clouds and the next land he saw were the islands in the bay as they approached Miami. He had a little time to wait after checking in at Aeronica, so he turned and followed the white line along the floor to the escalator and, when it finally deposited him in the main terminal a minute later, he felt he had been dropped into a new world. He had forgotten just how international the Miami terminal was, with all signs and public address announcements in both English and Spanish and with a multiracial stream of travelers moving in unbroken columns along the maze of corridors. He stopped to look around and, as he pulled to the side out of the flow of traffic, someone called to him close at hand, "Excuse me, sir, may I speak to you a moment?"

"What?" Hartley turned to face the short-haired young man who had spoken. "Yes, what is it?"

"Permit me to ask, sir, are you saved?"

"Saved...?" It was the boy's G.I. haircut that had tricked him. He paused, but only for a moment. "Habla Español?" Hartley said.

"What?"

Hartley kept a straight face at the boy's look of confusion. "Habla Español?"

"Er..., no..., that is...."

"Como...? Aqui en Miami y no Español? Es muy ridiculo, no? Adios." He chuckled to himself as he walked away, the blond gringo who speaks Spanish. The Jesus freaks had changed their uniform since last he had been approached, he thought, and now as Hartley looked ahead, he could spot them stationed every few yards along the concourse, clean faced, prep school type young men, the new soldiers for Christ with G.I. haircuts, each wearing a white shirt and carrying a book in his left hand. And then, just to his left, he heard the collision, running feet followed by the slap of leather on leather and the tinkle of coins and glass on the composition floor as a hurrying passenger crashed full force into a woman as she turned from the change booth.

"Oh my God!" the running passenger said. He was a young man in shorts and wearing a pack on his back. "Oh my God!" The woman was clearly stunned, holding up against the wall to keep from falling as her purse and valuables skittered across the floor. "Oh my God," the man in shorts said again. "...My plane, I'm about to miss my plane." And he ran on without another word.

"Here," Hartley said. He touched the woman's elbow to steady her. "You O.K.?"

"Yes..., yes, I think so."

He could see she had been badly shaken; her purse straps had been broken and the contents, including a handful of Nicaraguan córdobas and U.S. dollars, were blowing across the floor. "Let me catch this before it walks away," he said.

"Thank you," she said. She began to rally as he pushed some coins into a pile at her feet. "You're very kind."

Fragments of broken mirror rattled to the floor as he picked up her compact. "I'm afraid this won't be much use to you now."

"Oh no!" she said. "That was the last thing my husband gave me!" It was gold and engraved across the face with an Old English *K.K.* A trail of broken face powder sifted from it, perfuming the air.

"Maybe you can get the mirror replaced."

He reached for her notebook and the passport that lay open beside it: Karen Kellner, Washington, D.C. The cover was red. "Diplomatic corps?"

"Yes," she said. "Yes, I am." And he could not miss the finely-boned ankle that she placed firmly before him as she stooped to take her things.

"That guy gave you quite a jolt."

"If it hadn't been for the wall, I'd have gone down flat."

"Who was it who said, 'People are bloody ignorant savages?'"

She shook her head and limped slightly as he helped her to a nearby seat and, for the first time, he noticed the swollen red circle high on her cheekbone.

He touched the spot. "I'm afraid you're going to have a bruised cheek, too."

"Oh damn!"

"Wait here. I'll get some ice. Help keep the swelling down."

She was still obviously stunned, sitting as he had left her when he returned a few minutes later with the cup of ice from a nearby snack bar. "Hold this against your cheek," he said. "Maybe it won't turn blue."

"You're really very kind," she said. And then, just as he was about to ask where she was going, she looked at her watch and leapt to her feet. "Oh, my God! If I don't move, I'll have to run to catch *my* plane." She clutched her broken purse under one arm and shook his hand. "Thank you for everything," she said and walked away.

Her walk was strong, even with the slight limp, and he watched until she disappeared from view. "Very nice," he whispered. "Very nice." And then, as he turned back to the main concourse, all he could see were women. Where a few minutes earlier he had been studying the Jesus freaks and the signs and the multiracial flow of black, white, and mocha mobs, now he saw mainly the women: tall women, short women, bra-less women in T-shirts, women in shorts and stiletto heels, women in slacks, rich women in pearls and chic black sundresses, poor women with taped-together suitcases. The men just faded into the background. It was as though his vision had been suddenly changed or cleared, and he realized that, in most of the two years since his divorce from Diana, women had played almost no part in his life. He had been totally involved with financing and flying. Well, maybe now all that was changing, he thought. Maybe he was coming to life again.

7

The next time he saw Karen Kellner, she was walking down the ramp ahead of him to board the same Aeronica flight. He tried to reach her, but there were too many people in the way, and he was only able to catch up as he passed her first class seat on board the plane. "Hello, again," he said.

She seemed genuinely pleased to see him. "What a surprise," she said. "I almost went back to tell you. It was Beckett."

"Beckett? What was?"

The quote, 'People are bloody ignorant savages.' Except that Beckett said, 'People are bloody ignorant *apes*.'" She laughed and pointed to Hartley. "But not *all* people, thank God."

He wanted to linger, but other passengers were trying to push past, so he moved on. "See you in Managua," he called back and went to find his seat in the rear of the plane.

At least once, he tried to go back to see her in first class, but between the very efficient stewardess, who told him he was not allowed in first class, and the turbulence over the mountains, he had to wait until they landed in Managua and she was already on the ramp outside. He saw her ahead of him, still limping and carrying her broken purse under one arm and her teal shoulder bag over the other.

He reached her just as she stepped into the shadow of the terminal. "I see you're still able to make it," he said, and she was smiling as she turned.

"I was going to wait for you as soon as I got out of the sun," she said. "This heat is like a club!"

"Let me take your shoulder bag."

"No, no. I'll be fine," she said. "Don't want to become the total invalid."

"Let me see your cheek." He moved closer and lifted her chin. "Still a little red under the eye," he said. "But at least it's not turning blue."

"Thanks to you," Karen said, "you and the ice you brought me." And then as he released her chin, she looked up at the signs above them: *equipaje, aduana.* "Which way do we go here?"

"Right through there," Hartley said. "I think that's the passport booth at the end of the hall."

"There should be somebody here to meet me," Karen said. "Maybe we can give you a ride into town."

"That would be wonderful."

He followed her through passport control, noting for a second time that day the dark red color of her diplomatic passport as she laid it on the counter. And then he continued on behind her into the crowd beside the baggage carousel where, totally without warning, a man with a burr cut stepped suddenly from behind a post and took her arm.

Instinctively, she jerked free, but she obviously recognized the man as she turned to face him. "Rick! My God! You frightened me," she said. "I thought you were in Washington."

"I was," he said. He lifted the strap of her shoulder bag and looked down at her hip. "Why are you limping?"

"Somebody knocked me down in Miami."

"Knocked you down!"

"Some idiot running through the terminal. But here...," and she turned to Hartley, "... let me introduce you to the very kind man who helped me. Rick Adams, this is...." And then she faltered, laying her hand suddenly on Hartley's arm.

"Ron Hartley," he said as he shook hands with Rick Adams.

"Ron Hartley," she echoed. "He helped a lot. Picked me up, rounded up my things—even brought me ice for my bruises."

"You always were a good maiden in distress," Rick said.

"To hell with you," Karen said. She turned to pick up a suitcase as it came by on the conveyor belt. "Rick, why are you here?"

"Well, today I'm your driver."

"Good. Then we can give Ron a ride into town. But what I mean is, why are you in Managua? You didn't come all the way from Washington to be my driver."

"They needed a new security chief."

"You mean you're stationed here?"

"It was a last minute sort of thing."

"I hardly know what to say."

"Then today, somebody blew up the radio equipment here at the airport...."

"My God!"

"...So it didn't seem right for the cultural attaché to be met by nobody but a clerk."

"Sounds like I picked a great time to arrive."

"Think of it as a celebration in your honor," he said.

"What's going on?"

"We don't really know yet." He lifted her second suitcase off the conveyer, and the three of them walked out of the terminal, squinting in the heat that still radiated from the asphalt in spite of the dark clouds that had suddenly formed above the airport. "Now, Mr. Hartley, where are you going?"

"I'm staying at the Tropicana Hotel."

"The Tropicana?" Rick said. "That's unusual. Most visitors here like the Intercontinental."

"I remember the Tropicana from when I was a kid," Hartley said. "I lived here, and I always thought it was such a graceful old building."

Rick turned the ignition, and they started out of the parking lot. "You're not Nicaraguan?"

"No, no. U.S. My father worked here with American Fruit Company."

"That's a good outfit."

"Where did you two know each other?" Hartley said.

Karen turned in the front seat to look at him, and for the first time he noticed the dark green of her eyes. "We were in language school together," she said. She pointed to Rick, "And I thought this guy was going to a different duty station."

"You know how Uncle Sam is," Rick said.

"Yes, and I know how *you* are," she said.

"Well, I hope you both enjoy it," Hartley said.

They rode the rest of the way in silence until they reached the central plaza and Hartley got his first look at the ruined cathedral across from the *Palacio Nacional*. "My God," he said as they passed beside the old building, "what happened to it?" The twin towers were still standing, but there was no roof on the building and the façade had crumbled, leaving the front totally open. The tower clock was stopped at ten minutes after twelve.

"Earthquake," Rick said. "Four years ago, 1972, I think."

"I was still in Vietnam then," Hartley said.

"Did a lot of damage," Rick said.

"I didn't realize things were so bad here."

"You'll see lots of ruined buildings around. Looks like the place was bombed. I don't think *El Jefe* is very interested in repair work."

"El Jefe?"

"That's what folks here call the president."

"Oh."

"The cathedral's still beautiful though, isn't it?" Karen said. "In a spooky sort of way."

"Yes," Hartley said. "I always liked it." And then they were beneath the purple venenera flowers in front of the Tropicana Hotel.

"Here's your home away from home," Rick said.

Hartley gathered up his suitcase and shook hands with both of them. "Thanks so much for the lift."

"And thank you for all you did for me in Miami," Karen said.

"It was my pleasure, believe me. Maybe I'll see you again while I'm here. I know I've got to visit the embassy at some point."

"Call me if I can help," Karen said. She reached into her purse and handed him her card. "This is the embassy number. Call me."

And quickly she and Rick were gone, leaving Hartley alone before the white portico of the old hotel.

8

As it turned out, Hartley's very first call from the Tropicana Hotel was to the U.S. Embassy, but the line was busy, so he walked over to look out of his balcony window. Across a small courtyard, he could see the gilded façade of the National Theater and beyond it the central plaza and the battlements of the cathedral rising behind the *Palacio Nacional*. The aroma of roasting plantains drifted up from the street and, for a moment, he felt as though he might be ten again, still living here when his father had worked for American Fruit Company.

Then, as though waking suddenly, he turned back into the room toward the bed where he had been unpacking his suitcase and there, mixed in with his clothing, he saw a letter from Liliana Summerfield. He knew that Liliana had moved to Managua or San José, and he wanted to see her, but that would have to wait, he thought. Right now, he had to get on with it. He dumped the rest of his underwear into the dresser drawer, picked up the phone, and again dialed the embassy number from his notes on the bedside table—"Manuel Perez, Attaché for Labor and Domestic Relations, United States Embassy." And, at 10:30 the next morning, he walked into the foyer of the U.S. Embassy and presented his passport to the lone receptionist who sat like a bank teller behind darkly tinted glass. "I have an appointment with Mr. Perez," he said. "My name is Ronald Hartley."

It took only minutes for Mr. Perez to appear, a dark Hispanic man in a beige guayaberra pushing from behind the heavy steel door that served as the true threshold to the interior of the embassy. "Mr. Hartley?" he said. He offered his hand, speaking in polished North American English. "Come in. How can I help you?"

"I need an update," Hartley said.

"On what?"

"On a company known as Agri-21. My bank has been approached for a loan, and I need all the info I can get." He handed Perez a new card which identified him in embossed black letters as Foreign Investment Counselor for First International Bank.

"Who's the chief exec?"

"A man named Daniel Cortez," Hartley said.

"Ah," Perez said. He led the way into an office lined with gray file cabinets. "If you're interested in doing business with highly placed people, I don't think you could top it. He's the president's brother-in-law."

"Oh," Hartley said. "I didn't know. How's his business sense?"

"I'm not sure that question means the same thing here that it does in the States," Perez said. "He's the president's relative. He's covered. It would be very hard for his business to fail."

"That's nice," Hartley said. "But he's selling farm products on the international market. We'd hate to bed down with an idiot, even if he's got local connections."

"No problem." Perez reached for a folder from the file cabinet at his back. "He's got businesses all around. Hotels. Seafood. Even mining, I think. No problem at all. Have you met any of the top brass?"

"Not yet."

"Look here." Perez pushed the folder across his desk and pointed to the names at the top of a printout: Daniel Cortez, Fernando Cárdenas, Carlos Negroponte. "Cárdenas and Negroponte are vice presidents of the consortium," he said. "Negroponte is a colonel in the *Guardia*. Chief of Staff, I think.

"Really?"

Perez laughed. "This is a small country, Mr. Hartley. It's a rare army officer who isn't on the board of a corporation or two."

"Who is Cárdenas?"

"He's publisher of *El Tiempo*—the country's second largest newspaper."

"My God! Why do they need to borrow money?"

"Why use your own money if you can use somebody else's?" Perez said. "Besides, it probably costs less, and they'll get tax advantages for developing a new industry. Their government's very big on that sort of thing. And so are we, by the way."

"How do you happen to have all this information?"

"We're keeping track of how well this government keeps up with the new land reform laws we got them to make," Perez said. "We like to know who's doing what."

"I see," Hartley said. "And I guess, from my bank's point of view, if Agri-21 is backed by the government, the army, and the press, not much can really go wrong, can it?

"Not if the labor force is happy."

"Do you see a problem there?"

"Look," Perez said, "labor is always a problem—especially around here where somebody's always meddling with the laborers. But figures show the economy is strong, and the government's about as stable as any in the area, and these guys you're working with have got the best backing in the world."

"O.K.," Hartley said. "I just hope somebody in the company actually knows something about farming. But thanks." He offered his hand, and Perez walked with him down the hall toward the exit.

"Come back," Perez said. "Let me know how things go. We like to keep track of U.S. interests here."

Hartley was still thinking about Perez's story of army officers and politicians on the boards of corporations as he pushed through the crowd in the outer office of the embassy, and he didn't recognize Karen Kellner moving through the room in the opposite direction until she had already reached the interior security door, and there was nothing he could do but shout. "Wait," he said. "Karen, wait!"

She broke into a smile as she turned and let the security door slam behind her. "Hi!"

"I'm sorry to yell, but you were about to get away."

"What're you doing here?"

"I was trying to get some information from your industrial relations expert, Mr. Perez. How's your cheek?"

She offered him her hand. "My cheek's fine, thanks to you."

"Good. I'm glad." And then, without further hesitation, he said, "Would you have lunch with me?"

For an instant, her eyes shifted to the lone Marine and the woman receptionist who was watching her from the entrance, but then she looked back at Hartley and smiled. "Yes. Yes, of course."

They walked through the crowded streets and across the narrow causeway to the Tropicana Hotel, where they found a table beneath the arches of the white portico that extended across the entire front of the old building. "Oh, this is lovely." Karen said.

She pointed toward the theater, which Hartley could barely see through the purple flowers and the tangled branches of the Cruz de Cristo tree in the hotel courtyard. "I'm going to be spending lots of my time right next door to you," she said.

"Where? At the theater?"

"Yes. As cultural attaché. That theater is also the concert hall, lecture hall, art gallery—the works."

"I envy you."

"I'm excited about the possibilities. I really am." She looked back at Hartley. "But what was that you said at the embassy—you were doing something in industrial relations?"

"It's a long story," Hartley said. "For the second time in my life, I've become a banker."

"What were you before that?"

"A soldier...a pilot." He heard her sudden intake of breath, but he went on. "Since the war, I've been part owner of a small airline, but we ran into trouble. You know what a mess the U.S. economy is in, with interest running eighteen to twenty percent...." He realized she was looking down at the table. "What's the matter?'

"Did you fly in the army?"

"That's where I learned. U.S. Army. Vietnam, '68 to '70. And again in '71 to '72." Suddenly she was looking out beyond the white column toward the thorns of the Cruz de Cristo tree. "Did I say something wrong?"

She looked back. "No. I'm sorry. Did you ever know an army officer named Robin Kellner in Vietnam?"

"No," Hartley said. "I didn't."

"He was my husband." She paused. "He went down in a helicopter ... with his whole platoon ... upside-down in a rice paddy in '71."

"I'm sorry," Hartley said. "It was a bad time."

"I know I've had a good six years to get over that, but some things don't get neatly buried the way we'd like. I was also pregnant with his child—which I lost two weeks after I got the news of Robin's death. So, all in all...," she looked directly into his eyes and smiled, "...I am not neutral about the army or army aviation. It's almost like the six years had never passed."

"I'm glad you told me." He touched her hand on the table, but she moved it away. "Well, for me," Hartley said, "at this point, I'm ex-army, ex-pilot, and ex-spouse. Not all entirely by choice, mind you, but for all practical purposes, you could call me Mr. Ex."

She laughed, and then they were both laughing as the waiter approached with their lunch.

9

When Hartley returned to his room after lunch, he sat for a time on the edge of the bed staring at the opposite wall and thinking about Karen Kellner. Lovely woman, he thought, but don't take her too seriously. One minute, she seems open to new attachments, the next minute, she isn't. Stay tuned, but don't take her too seriously.

He had business to take care of. The first thing on his list was to call Daniel Cortez at Agri-21, but he was frustrated at every attempt. "El Señor Cortez no esta aqui," the secretary finally told him. "He isn't here, and we don't know when he'll return."

So he left a message and paced to the window. From the courtyard, he could hear the blackbirds singing in the trees. Maybe he should go out and join them, he thought, maybe get a newspaper, or at least get some exercise.

By the time he returned to the sleepy lobby of the old hotel thirty minutes later, the climate of the place was changed. The staff seemed more attentive, and the clerk recognized him even before he reached the desk. "Ah, Señor Hartley...." His voice seemed strangely excited. "Señor Cortez has been trying to reach you. He wants you to join him for dinner at 7:30. His driver will pick you up." The clerk executed a sharp about-face and handed him a note from the mailbox along with his key. "Is there anything else I can do for you, sir?"

"Er, no. Thank you."

Even the elevator man seemed changed, leaping from his stool and standing almost at attention as Hartley approached. "Buenas tardes, Señor."

"Yes. Good afternoon."

"I hope you enjoy your stay with us, sir." He held the door for Hartley at the third floor. "And if there is any other way I may serve you, please let me know."

"Yes, I will."

Hartley looked again at the clerk's note as he moved down the hall toward his room: "Sr. Daniel Cortéz y Saavedra wishes you to join him and the officers of Agri-21...." The clerk had written out the full name, and Hartley was no longer a casual guest at the hotel. Maybe this was what Perez had meant about Cortez: "He's the president's brother-in-law. He's covered."

He was ready by 7:20, suit, tie, and the banker's smile of understanding, practiced at least twice before the mirror. And he barely had time to glance more than once through the window at the sharply uniformed guards patrolling the plaza before the clock above the National Theater began to chime the half hour, and he heard a restrained tapping at his door.

It was the uniformed chauffeur. "Señor Hartley?"

"Yes."

Daniel Cortez was waiting in his limousine, sitting back against the cushions with the relaxed ease, Hartley thought, of a man long accustomed to money and power. "Ah, Mr. Hartley, welcome to our country." Speaking a darkly musical English, he offered his soft hand in the glare of the dome light. "It's good of you to travel all this way on our behalf."

"I hope it'll be the beginning of a long partnership," Hartley said.

"Yes, I hope so. Now. The particulars...." The driver started the engine and moved into the street as Hartley settled back. "The central part of our city has its charm," Cortez said, "but it is still badly damaged from the earthquake that struck in '72. Tonight, I would like to take you to the modern part...," Cortez laughed slightly, "...to show you that Managua is not just the sleepy

Spanish town it's been made out to be." He leaned across Hartley and pointed through the window to the lights on the rim of the hills. "Up there—the Mayan Plaza Hotel—but you will see."

In the higher elevations, they moved along quiet avenues lined with large homes, stone fences, and cast iron gates. "This is the new city," Cortez said. "And this is what I hope you will remember—no matter what you see elsewhere. This is the prosperous direction of the future."

"Looks very comfortable," Hartley said.

"Oh yes. With all our natural resources, there is no reason why Nicaragua should not become the garden spot of the western hemisphere."

By then they had reached the hotel, and in the lights before the broad entrance, uniformed attendants were opening the doors and greeting Cortez with shouts of welcome. "Bienvenido, Señor! Adelante!"

It was like the arrival of a movie star or a general, Hartley thought, military guards with submachine guns across their chests braced on each side of the main door as the hotel manager pushed forward to meet Cortez. "Colonel Negroponte and Señor Cárdenas are waiting for you in the casino, Señor."

"Excellent," Cortez said. "Thank you, Franco." He patted the manager's shoulder as Franco turned to lead the way.

They passed through the crowded lobby and continued down the stairs, descending past a fountain, past golden cages of exotic birds and down still another flight until they came to a gilded doorway with the sign inlaid above: *Casino.*

"Your friends are at the roulette tables," the manager said.

Cortez patted his shoulder again as the manager departed, and for a moment they stood in the doorway, adjusting to the brilliant light and the rattle of gambling machines. "Now, where can they be playing?"

Beyond the nearest bank of slot machines, Hartley could see roulette wheels, blackjack tables, dice, and other games he could not identify. But, as they moved further into the room, a woman's voice called suddenly from behind, "Daniel!" and both men turned as the most beautiful woman Hartley had ever seen approached Cortez. "Daniel," she said again. "Daniel, where have you been hiding? Why have you not been to visit us?" She embraced Cortez and kissed his cheek and seemed to press his elbow into her bosom as she took his arm to usher him forward. She could have been any race or nationality, Hartley thought, Eurasian, Mestizo, Mulatto, Italian, a blend of all races and nations. Her hair seemed dark, and yet, unmistakable flashes of gold reflected from it as she moved beneath the light.

Cortez switched from Spanish to English as he gestured toward Hartley, "Oriana, this is my guest, Ronald Hartley. Treat him nicely."

"Delighted, Mr. Hartley," Oriana said. Her hand was cool. "I hope you will visit us often."

"Er, yes. Thank you," Hartley said.

She laughed and again took Cortez's arm. "I know Colonel Negroponte is to meet you for dinner," she said, "but he has become obsessed with roulette." The crowd parted for her as she urged the two men forward. "I hope you can take him away before he breaks the bank."

Hartley could identify Colonel Negroponte in dress uniform beside the roulette table as she pointed. The game squares of the table were nearly invisible beneath stacks of silver chips, and the croupier was waiting while the colonel stood to one side reviewing his strategy like a field commander. "My God!" Hartley whispered at the sight of the fortune on the table. And then he realized that the colonel had given a sign and everyone else had fallen silent.

For an instant, the croupier's eyes met Oriana's before he looked impassively away at the far wall and sent the tiny white ball whirling around the rim of the wheel. For a long time, the ball seemed suspended in its arc, but gradually it slowed, dropped lower in the wheel and began to bounce across the serrations until it finally came to rest on RED 2, and a shout of applause rose from around the table. Colonel Negroponte raised his hands above his head and gave a little dance like a victorious prize fighter as the croupier began pushing a large pile of chips into his corner.

"Congratulations, Carlos," Cortez said. "You should have an excellent appetite."

"How much was that?" Hartley whispered to Oriana.

She touched his arm, holding the question until after she had spoken to the croupier, speaking suddenly very rapidly and confidentially in Spanish before turning and smiling again to Hartley, "Oh, about 50,000 córdobas all told, about 25,000 U.S. dollars."

"On one throw!?" Hartley exclaimed.

But Oriana was now embracing the colonel, kissing his cheek. "Carlos, you devil!" she said. "You've been trying to do that for years. If you keep on, you'll put me out of business."

"Oh no, my beautiful one," Colonel Negroponte said. "Never would I allow you to be put out of business. I keep hoping that one day I will be truly lucky and find *you* among my winnings."

"You know I never gamble," Oriana said.

"Oh no," the colonel said. "Of course not." A loud laugh went up from the men standing near. "How could I make such a mistake?" And then, amid the laughter, Daniel Cortez brought Hartley forward to begin introductions

"Ah, Mr. Hartley," the colonel said, "we've been expecting you. And, obviously, your presence here tonight brought me good luck." Oriana was still hanging on his arm, but he reached back and stopped a waiter carrying a tray of drinks. "A toast," the colonel shouted as he lifted glasses from the tray. "On this great night—a toast to Oriana, who has kept the gambling wheels honest; and a toast to our guest and his good luck, to Ronald Hartley and the First International Bank!"

10

"It was a case of desperation," Cortez had said at dinner. "Agri-21 was the result of sheer desperation." But as Hartley returned alone, sunk in the deep cushions of Cortez's limousine, it seemed laughable to think of Cortez being desperate about anything—Cortez receiving his welcome at the door of the hotel, Cortez moving through the glitter of the casino with Oriana on his arm. Desperate? For the moment, Hartley had trouble thinking of anything but Oriana's perfect face. If this was desperation, then there should be more of it. The driver stopped for a group of people crowding into a small bus at the station on Cortazar Street and then moved on slowly to the hotel.

It had been Reynaldo Cárdenas, the newspaper publisher, who tried to explain. Cárdenas had been the quietest of the three Agri-21 executives, sitting back at dinner between the colonel and Cortez, relaxed with the light shining on his white forelock as he sipped his brandy. "In many ways, Agri-21 was inspired by your government," he said to Hartley.

"How?"

"Through their insistence on land reform. When the laws were passed, we realized that, unless we used our land for agriculture, it would be constantly under assault, maybe taken from us."

"To be used by peasants?"

"Yes." Cárdenas had laughed. "Now none of us had ever been especially interested in farming. But when it became a question of farming or losing the lands of our fathers to a group of Mestizos and Indians—well...," he laughed again, "...we developed a monumental love of agriculture. Out of desperation, as Daniel says. We now have 15,000 acres under cultivation, and we hope to have much more."

"This is why we need machinery as soon as we can get it," Colonel Negroponte said. "Expansion."

"But not only that, Carlos." Cárdenas had taken a long pull on his brandy. "Let us be frank, Mr. Hartley. And this is a thing that should reassure you and the officers of your bank. A tractor is much less trouble than a man. Even without expansion, why should we hire hundreds of lazy and ignorant *compesinos* when we can do the same work with fifty technicians and twenty tractors?"

"It sounds like good economy to me," Hartley said. "Will I be able to see these lands?"

"Yes, of course. We want to show you everything. Tomorrow, if that is all right with you. We have excellent managers on each of our *fincas*, our farms, who can explain the technical details."

———

Hartley thanked the driver as they reached the Tropicana Hotel, and he was thinking again of Oriana's face as he entered the lobby and disturbed the drowsing night clerk from his chair behind the front desk. "Oh yes! Mr. Hartley." The clerk suddenly sprang to life and pulled a piece of yellow notepaper from the box along with the key. "You have a message from the U.S. Embassy."

"I do?" Hartley looked at the note. "Call Karen Kellner," it said. And there was a number at the embassy. He thanked the clerk and crammed the note into his pocket as he moved toward the elevator. He had not thought of Karen for four hours, and now, after seeing Oriana, he felt unsure about calling her at all. But still, after breakfast the next morning, he made the call. Again sitting on the edge of his bed, he dialed and waited through four rings and a Spanish-speaking secretary, until Karen came to the phone. "Oh," she said. "Hi. I'm glad you called. I was just rushing out. Let me tell you what I had in mind. There's a young playwright named

Tomás Rubio. He has a play opening tonight, and I've got to see it. Starts at eight o'clock. I thought you might like to see it, too."

"Sounds great. But I have to go out of town today, to Baná, and I don't know how far that is...."

"It's only the next province over—a few miles."

"Then I should be able to get back in time, but I can't be sure, so if you want to make other plans...."

"That's all right. I'll risk it."

"Is the play at the National Theater?"

"No. At a private club. He's known for his folk plays, and we may want him as part of our cultural exchange program. I've got to make a recommendation."

"I'll call when I get back, but if I don't make it by seven o'clock, you'll know I've been tied up."

"Let me give you my number."

"Ahh!" Hartley said as he hung up. "Ah! Now that's better." And then he began to whistle the tune of "I Believe in Yesterday" as he continued dressing for his trip to Agri-21.

It was the pistol beneath Cortez's left arm that changed Hartley's mood thirty minutes later. He had followed the chauffeur through the lobby and entered the limousine at the curb, and, as Cortez leaned forward to shake hands, Hartley saw the flash of leather and gun metal beneath his jacket. It was like seeing a man with his fly open or with egg on his cheek and, for a long time after their first greeting; Hartley could think of almost nothing to say in response to Cortez's running commentary.

"On your right is Xhictocol Crater," Cortez said as they reached the outskirts of the city. He leaned over and pointed down the steep ravine to the circular blue lake several hundred feet below. "They say the volcano has been extinct for a thousand years." But Hartley only grunted and nodded, now newly aware of the heavy movement of Cortez's jacket. "From this point on, perhaps for twenty miles, you will see the lands of the American Fruit Company."

"I want to visit them while I'm here," Hartley said finally. "My father worked for them once back in the forties."

"Ah, that will be easy," Cortez said. "I know the Kingstons well. Mrs. Kingston is a member of our board." He pointed to a small gauge railroad track which ran parallel to the highway. "That's their railroad," he said. "But it's very important to us at Agri-21. It's our main line from the fields to the ocean and world markets."

"Very convenient."

"They give us good shipping rates," Cortez said. He laughed. "So long as we don't ship bananas and other fruits to compete with them. Then, they might not be so friendly."

"Is there no other rail line?"

"It would seem silly to build another line right beside an existing one, don't you think?"

Cortez sat back, but beneath his loose coat, Hartley could again see the bulge of the holster, and he spoke suddenly, quickly, as though hurrying to get rid of the question: "Why do you carry a gun?"

Cortez looked straight ahead, continuing his conversation as though he hadn't heard the question. "We worked out a careful agreement with American Fruit before we began operations," he said. "Using their rail line makes profit for them as well as for us."

Hartley spoke louder. "Should I carry a pistol?"

"Mr. Hartley...." Cortez sighed. "There are some conditions in Nicaragua that are very sad. I'm sorry I was so careless and spoiled your otherwise perfect day."

"But should I carry arms?"

"No. Certainly not when you're with me." Cortez leaned forward to release the catch of a drawer beneath the front seat, and Hartley looked down to see two submachine guns and two pistols, carefully oiled and lying in neat parallel rows. "When you travel with me, you are amply covered."

"But why?" Hartley said.

"I am the president's brother-in-law," Cortez said. "You know yourself, in the States, the assassination of leaders, threats to their families—even the recent threat against President Ford." He closed the drawer of machine guns. "The same is true here."

"President Somoza is taking steps to correct the old situation here, isn't he?"

"Oh yes. Of course. But old grudges die hard. The president's own father was assassinated only twenty years ago, if you remember. And I...," Cortez patted the bulge beneath his arm, "...I prefer to be prepared. When the chips are really down, one can rely only on oneself."

"I certainly agree with that," Hartley said.

"Good. I knew you were a practical man." Cortez smiled now. "Do you ride horseback, Mr. Hartley?"

"Well, yes. But it's been years."

"I've called my manager to have horses ready."

"I'm hardly dressed for it."

"Oh, we won't go far. But it makes the trip across muddy fields much easier. They're really my wife's horses, but she likes to have us ride them."

"Your wife—the president's sister?"

"Yes."

They were well out of the hills now, driving beside the river and a broad plain of cultivated fields. "Here you see the beginning of our lands," Cortez said. "Cotton, tobacco, sugar cane, many other things. In the hills, of course, there is coffee."

"Where is your market for tobacco?"

"Oh, the States, of course," Cortez said. "It nearly all goes to the States. The quality is just as good as what you grow there, but the cost—that is another matter. We really have no competition when it comes to cost."

The driver slowed and turned now off the paved road between a set of stone pillars and a concrete guardhouse where two guards were lounging in the front seat of a black sports van beside the road. The men sprang quickly to their feet, unslinging their carbines and submachine guns as the car stopped at the gate. "Oh, Señor Cortez!" the guard leader said as he approached the window.

"Good morning, Zia," Cortez said. He shook hands and spoke in

Spanish through the car window. "How are you?"

"Very fine, Señor."

"And the family? That new son of yours, how is he doing?"

"Oh, he's wonderful, Señor. Really growing. Going to be quite a man."

"I bet he will be, with you as his dad." Cortez continued in a joshing, playful tone, "Any more on the way?"

"Well, you know how it is, Señor."

"Zia, you devil! You mean your poor wife is expecting again?"

"No Señor. Not my wife, my girlfriend."

"Zia!" The two men laughed. "You *are* a devil!" Cortez touched Hartley with his elbow. "This is why we keep him as head of our guards, more *cajones* than he knows what to do with." The three men laughed again. "Just keep them all well and happy, Zia. Well and happy. And don't let them weaken you."

"I'll do my best, Señor."

"Listen, we'll be here for about the next hour," Cortez said.

"Very good, Señor. Just call me, if you need anything." Zia threw a crisp salute and signaled the others to raise the barrier bar so the car could continue forward.

"More automatic weapons," Hartley said.

"Yes," Cortez said. "Part of the cost of success, I'm afraid."

They rode on horseback across the finca with the manager whose name was Corico, riding across the soft ground where hundreds of men were working to prepare for new planting and then on to the packing houses where both men and women worked to wash and prepare vegetables for shipping. "Here, too, you see our methods are rather primitive," Cortez said. He spoke again in Spanish so Corico could join them. "What would you do, if you had grading equipment, Corico?"

"Oh, Señor, we could double production—get more to market before it spoils."

"Ah, and if you had twenty tractors—harvesters?"

Both men began laughing. "Señor, there is no limit!" Corico

turned to Hartley, rising for a moment in a cascade of Spanish that Hartley could hardly follow. "No limit. And I would no longer have to fight with the men—just put gas in the tractor and drive it toward the field!"

But it was the tobacco operation that interested Hartley most. The crop was coming in, and the workers were using mules and hanging sleds to take the leaves to the curing barn. "It looks like home," he said. "But I haven't seen this kind of operation since I was a kid."

"We need so badly to improve the equipment and update our methods," Cortez said. "But, of course, tobacco will always require heavy labor."

"It's always been a big money crop in my part of the world."

"Yes," Cortez said, "but the center of industry changes. And your bank is smart enough to see that. I'm sure you'll agree that finally you have to let the market dictate your financial decisions."

It was a phrase that Hartley had heard often during his student years, "Let the market dictate." But now, as he dismounted and followed Cortez through the curing barns, the words took on a strange new significance that he didn't fully understand. And he was still thinking about them two hours later in the limousine as they wound again along the clay and gravel road back toward the guardhouse and saw the group of *campesinos* standing by the roadway. "What is this?" Cortez said. He leaned forward in the seat, and Hartley could see his hand clearly as he reached beneath his coat to unsnap the strap of the pistol. "Wait for me," Cortez said. But Hartley ignored him and followed two steps behind as Cortez paced briskly toward the guardhouse. "Zia, what is it?"

"These men want to see you, Señor. They've come with their pastor."

"Why? Do they want a prayer service?'

"No, Señor. He's their spokesman, Pastor Quetoda. Shall I run them off?"

"No, wait." Cortez looked beyond the guard and laughingly singled out the one man who obviously was different from the others. "Pastor Quetoda," he called. "What's the matter? Are you not busy enough with the souls of your parishioners?"

"Si, Señor. But I'm concerned with all the business of God's kingdom."

"Then you're a very busy man," Cortez said. "And I suggest you let us handle our part while you go mind God's business elsewhere."

"My parishioners work for you, Señor."

"Then, I'm counting on you to keep them honest."

"Señor, it is a question of pay for extra night work in the tobacco barns," Quetoda said.

"Night work's part of the job."

"Si. But, after they have worked in the field all day, it's only fair. It takes them away from their families and gives them no time to work their own gardens."

"Tell them if they can find higher wages from another employer, they're welcome to go."

"We ask you to consider this, Señor. We'll talk again, after you've had time to think."

"I've given my answer already."

Quetoda turned back toward the men at the rusty pickup truck beside the road, but he stopped after two steps and looked again at Cortez. "One other thing, Señor. The men have heard rumors that you plan to replace them with tractors and machinery. Is this true?"

"Where did you hear this?"

"As I said, it's rumor."

"Then tell the men if they do their work and don't cause trouble, their jobs are safe. I don't have new tractors or machinery." He laughed. "Tell them they can sleep peacefully at night—unless they're working in the tobacco barns." Cortez came back to the limousine then, grabbing Zia by the arm as he came. "Get me the names of all those men," he said, speaking now not six inches from Zia's face. "And then get them out of here," he said. "Get rid of them. Life is too short to deal constantly with troublemakers." He signaled to the driver, and the limousine lurched suddenly forward, squealing its tires as it reached the concrete and continued to accelerate. "I'm sorry that you had to be troubled with this, Mr.

Hartley," he said. "But it goes with directing a company."

"De nada," Hartley said. He shrugged. "It's nothing."

11

But it *was* something. Just what, Hartley didn't know, but on his return to the city, it became another thing that robbed him of words—like the pistol beneath Cortez's coat. Surely, Cortez had not lied to the men, but his deception was unmistakable. "What will those men do when you finally bring in tractors?" Hartley had asked him.

But Cortez had just looked at him blankly, as though he didn't understand the question. "I suppose they'll have more time to tend their gardens," he had said.

But for Hartley that was no answer at all, and the question was still bothering him when he reached the hotel and found a message to call Brad at the bank. He went directly to his room, planning to make the call immediately, but instead, he just sat for a time by the window looking out at the strollers in the plaza. If an employer would deceive his workers, would he also deceive his financial backers? he wondered. And was it a financial problem or a labor problem or an ethical problem? Was it a problem at all? He couldn't quite be sure, but he was going to have to give some coherent account to Brad and the bank very quickly.

He waited another minute. First, he would call Karen, he thought. And he reached her on the second ring. "I'm back," he said.

"Great!" she said. "The theater is at 8:30."

"Why don't we meet for dinner at seven?"

"That would be nice. I'll meet you in the hotel lobby."

"Wonderful."

Her energetic and efficient tone somehow made him smile as he hung up. "We'll see," he said to himself. "We'll see. But don't count on anything."

He sighed, waited still another moment, then dialed the international code for the States where Brad answered and responded with audible excitement in his voice. "Ronnie! It's good to hear you at last. What's the news?"

"I've just spent two days with the people at Agri...."

But Brad had no patience at all for preliminaries. "Hell, what I really want to know is, are they solvent?" he said. "Just tell me that."

"Oh yes, they're solvent. Very solvent."

"Great!"

"I would guess they've got a line to the national treasury, if they want it."

"So what's your recommendation?"

"I think I recommend going forward with the loan."

"Why are you hesitant?"

"Because, first, if they do it right, they're going to need a lot more equipment and a lot more money than they're requesting," Hartley said. "The final amount should be closer to ten million than one million."

"So much the better, if they're sound."

"We need to decide how to negotiate that."

"O.K. Yes. I agree. But I don't want to wait any longer on this tractor business. The dealer defaulted on another payment today."

"Oh."

"We're losing thousands and he's threatening to go bankrupt and leave us holding the bag entirely."

"Well, we sure don't want that."

"You're damn right, we don't."

"But listen. There's one thing that worries me here."

"What?"

"Their labor policies. I mean, Brad, Agri-21 is feudal. The bosses are barely out of the middle ages. But the workers are in the twentieth century. They've got a union and they're hungry."

"That's not our problem," Brad said. "Not if the company's solvent."

"They're gonna put a lot of people out of work around here if they get those tractors."

"And they're gonna put a lot of people out of work around *here* if they don't," Brad said. "Starting with you and me."

For a moment, Hartley was silent. "What happens if those dismissed workers get mad and decide to close down the operation? Where's our money then?"

"Listen, Ron, we can't solve every potential economic and political problem. All we can do is take reasonable precautions. They've got a government and a police force. The State Department says the government's solid, and you say the company's solid. I say we go ahead."

"Yes. O.K. I do, too. For the one million, two hundred thousand. I'll get back to you about the rest."

"Just don't let your damn sentimental streak get in the way."

"What are you talking about?"

"I'm talking about your tendency to sympathize with whoever looks like the underdog."

"Brad, I've been there. I know what it feels like to have your work disappear from right in front of your face."

"That's what I mean. It's *your* problem, not the bank's problem."

"I hate to do it to somebody else."

"You won't be doing it to somebody else. You'll be bringing their economy into the twentieth century. You'll be protecting our investors."

"O.K."

"You'll help produce food for a hungry world."

"O.K."

"Keep on saying it to yourself, if you have to: 'I'm helping produce food for a hungry world....' Anything. But remember your priorities, for God's sake. Find a buyer for those tractors. Make a client for the bank."

12

Hartley was still worrying about the relation between labor policy and income when he came downstairs an hour later, after his conversation with Brad, but it took only one glance at Karen Kellner in the lobby to refocus his mind entirely. She was sitting beside the cage of jungle birds in the center of the room and, when she stood to greet him, he felt a small explosion of excitement in the pit of his stomach. White pumps, lace lining the V neck of her silk blouse, a soft knit shawl to protect her shoulders from the night air, and a certain unmistakable North American vitality in her movements as she stepped forward, offering her hand, greeting him almost musically. "Hello again!" she said.

Hartley folded her hand warmly between both of his as he nodded toward the dining room. "I've made reservations for dinner on the veranda."

"Wonderful."

"Yes, it is wonderful, especially after the day I've had today," Hartley said, and he began to tell her about his visit to Agri-21 and his concern for the campesinos. "I hope this play we're going to see is a comedy."

But the play was not a comedy, although their effort to find the theater reduced them to laughter several times. First, the taxi took them to Avenida del Mayo Norte instead of Avenida del Mayo Sur. Then, in the dimly lit streets, they stumbled twice into the wrong gates and the wrong courtyards before finally opening the door into the red and black interior of The Club La Ronde where the performance was about to begin.

"I don't know anything about this play," Karen said as they found their seats, "but Tomás Rubio is probably the best known Latin American playwright today."

"I hope I can follow the language."

"His specialty is folk plays. I saw one in Mexico City last year," she said.

However, *this* play, entitled "La Fuerza," was not a folk play at all, and it was highly disturbing to Hartley from the opening curtain. In a stylized and surrealistic way, it told the story of the celebrated bandit Pepe Reynaldo, and it began with the graphic rape of Pepe's wife by a Guardia officer who, when he turned his back to the audience revealed a U.S. flag sewn across his tunic.

The effect on Hartley was instantaneous. His heart was suddenly pounding very hard, and he was hot around the ears, and it was only seconds before he turned to Karen and touched her arm. "Let's get out of here."

"What?"

"I don't see any point in watching the U.S. get insulted."

"But it's my job," Karen said. "I have to know what they're saying."

"I think it's very obvious what they're saying, and I don't want to hear it."

"Then, goodbye," she said. "I'm going to watch."

"You mean you're staying?"

"Yes."

Karen placed a finger to her lips as she looked back at the stage, and for a moment, he hunched forward in his seat, undecided whether to sit and suffer through the obvious propaganda for "educational purposes" or to stand and stomp out with indignation. But finally, the idea of deserting his date at the theater just didn't feel right, and he sat back. Maybe the play would get better.

But, if anything, the play got worse as it told how a brutal government, backed by the United States, had exploited the family of Pepe Reynaldo and the people of Nicaragua. There was no alternative except through revolution, the play seemed to say, and it closed with a rousing exhortation for the audience to rise and fight for Liberty and Justice and the freedom of Pepe Reynaldo and all the nation.

By the final curtain, Hartley was in a rage, but the audience around him stood and shouted with delight. They cheered and threw kisses to the actors. They stomped their feet and clapped, leaving Hartley and Karen alone on a gringo island of non-appreciation.

"God!" Hartley said. "There's no doubt what camp we're in tonight."

"He never did that before," Karen said. "Rubio never wrote like that before. This is something totally new."

And then, as the applause began to wane, the entire room was suddenly flooded with brilliant white light, and a bull horn was blaring an order for silence as armed Guardia soldiers pounded down the aisles and charged onto the stage to grab the actors and throw both men and women against the painted flats.

"Silence!" came the shout from the loud-speaker. "Silence! This is Captain Segura speaking. The Club La Ronde is hereby declared illegal and every person in this building is under arrest."

People in the audience began shouting back at the captain, and Hartley took the moment of confusion to grab Karen's hand and pull her toward the exit, pushing through the crowd with his shoulder like a football guard. "No! Wait!" Karen shouted behind him.

But Hartley pushed on. "Come on," he said. "They can't arrest us. We're American citizens."

"Will you wait!"

Suddenly she grabbed his jacket and turned him with surprising strength as the voice on the loudspeaker blared again at his back: "Stop where you are and put your hands on your heads!"

"They'll let us go as soon as they see our passports," Karen said.

"You, maybe. You're with the embassy."

"And you're with me."

"Stop where you are and place your hands on your heads," the loudspeaker said again. "Anyone attempting to escape will be shot!"

"Do what they tell you," Karen said. She put her hands on her head and, in an instant, she was separated from him and calling over the heads of people who had slipped between. "If you try to resist, they may shoot you first and *then* look at your passport."

The order for silence came again as Captain Segura walked on stage dressed in combat fatigues and carrying a bull horn. "Move quietly in single file to the rear door," he said. "Follow our orders and you will not be hurt."

Hartley followed Karen's example then, moving with hands on his head toward the guards at the door where he could see vans being loaded with prisoners. "This is ridiculous," he said. And then, as he reached the door, he lowered his arms and said it again loudly in Spanish to the soldier in charge. "This is ridiculous! I'm an American citizen." To which the soldier's only response was an upward stroke with the butt of his carbine, bouncing the blow off Hartley's shoulder but cracking the side of his skull hard enough to send him sprawling onto the floor between two other soldiers who quickly picked him up by belt and collar and hurled him face down onto the floor of the waiting van.

13

He did not pass out, but he was groggy, and by the time he had pulled himself upright to avoid being crushed in the press of people, the truck was moving, and Hartley had totally lost track of Karen. He touched the lump that was rising on the side of his head, and his fingers came away sticky in the darkness. "Where are we going?" He spoke in Spanish to the man beside him. "Where are they taking us?"

"No sé," the man said. "It is anyone's guess."

Hartley reached for his handkerchief and pressed it to the cut on his head, and as he did, the truck began swaying, throwing the standing prisoners from side to side as it rounded sharp curves at high speed. "Oh God!" some woman said in the darkness, "Oh Jesus! Oh Mary! Oh save us!"

The woman was too short even to be seen above the shoulders around her, and Hartley wondered again where Karen was. He had heard rumors of the Guardia's treatment of women. And certainly the play had left nothing to the imagination. Damn stubborn woman! he thought. Damn stubborn woman! And then he grabbed the walls for balance as the truck swerved again several times in quick succession before it finally slowed and braked sharply, throwing the prisoners screaming and clawing into a crush against the forward wall.

"Everybody out!" The doors were jerked open and blinding lights engulfed them as the command came again. "Everybody out." From the dark interior of the truck, Hartley could see that it was the same officer as at the theater, parading back and forth behind the trucks with his bullhorn at the ready. "Stand against the stone wall." The captain was the only one who spoke, while the guards gave their own directions with shoves and prods and the blows of rifle butts until all the prisoners were herded into a line. "Against the stone wall! Against the stone wall!"

Behind them, the steel doors of the compound slammed shut as the captain strode to the center of the yard. He was smiling and switching his leg with his swagger stick like the ringmaster of a circus. "What a field day!" he said. "What a triumph!" He pointed to the line of prisoners. "The cream of anarchy in Nicaragua, the elite of revolution! Now you know who runs our country. Don't you?" He nodded with satisfaction as he surveyed them. "Who?" he shouted. "Tell me, who runs Nicaragua?"

He waited for a moment in silence until someone said, "The Guardia," very weakly.

"What? Who? I can't understand you. Guards, help them. Who runs Nicaragua?"

The answer came loudly in unison from the guards, "The Guardia *Nacional!*"

"Who?"

"The Guardia Nacional, sir!"

"Right! Now let's see if our guests understand this." Captain Segura pointed his swagger stick at a small man on the left flank. "*You,* who runs Nicaragua?"

The man looked down at the ground and mumbled.

"What? I can't hear you."

One of the guards pushed the prisoner harshly forward so that he stumbled to his knees. "Answer the captain."

"Stand up and tell me clearly who runs Nicaragua."

"The Guardia Nacional," the man said.

"Good. Tell the rest of these people."

The man turned to the line of prisoners, and his voice cracked as he shouted, "The Guardia Nacional!"

"Right. Now, let's have a test." Segura began pointing to other prisoners in the line and repeating the question. "You..., you...,

you..., who runs Nicaragua?" Until he came to Karen standing just in from the left end of the line: "And you, Señorita? Surely you know who runs Nicaragua."

She did not hesitate, her voice ringing strongly through the courtyard, "I am an American citizen on a diplomatic mission, and I have no opinion about politics in Nicaragua!"

Captain Segura stopped, his face sobering for just a moment before he regained his smile and spoke in careful English. "Then welcome to Nicaragua, Señorita. I'm sure tonight you have received a graphic political education." He shouted to the guards, "Put these people in a cell and bring this woman to my office." Then he executed a sharp about face and disappeared through the nearest door.

The prisoners were herded into a long hall, where they were divided and crowded into holding cells that were too small to allow anyone to sit. When the doors clanged shut, Hartley just stood unmoving, wedged upright in the press of bodies. Someone close by had lost control of his bowels, and now that odor nearly made him gag as it mingled with the smell of sweat and fear in the unventilated room.

The lump on his head was throbbing painfully and, when he was finally able to raise his hand from his side to press against it, he could feel moisture around the cut and dried blood down the back of his neck. The man beside him moaned as though in pain, swaying with his eyes closed. God! It was all so ridiculous, Hartley thought. Through all of his military service, though people had certainly shot at him, he had led a charmed life, never wounded, never captured, never even deprived of his rations for more than half a day. But now....

The man beside him moaned again in his ear, and Hartley realized that the man had already passed out but couldn't fall because his body was so tightly wedged between the others. God! Hartley thought, keep your circulation going. And gradually the unconscious man began to sink, going to his knees and then down, doomed to be crushed unless relief came soon.

Hartley's feet and ankles were already numb and he began to

wiggle his toes and fingers. Somehow, he had to keep the system working. Outside, he could hear guards in the hall and keys against the barred doors, and he began to shout. "Médico! Médico! Necesitamos un médico!"

Gradually others in the cell began to raise the cry along with him, and to Hartley's surprise, two guards suddenly appeared and asked what the problem was. "This man is dying," Hartley said.

There was a sudden flurry of motion, and the guards opened the door while the prisoners pushed the man's body toward the front where it fell and the guards dragged it to the center of the hall. "He'll be all right," the sergeant of the guard said. And then he looked at the clipboard in his hand and scanned the cell. "Which one of you is Señor Hartley?"

The sergeant led him out, flanked by two armed guards as they moved across the courtyard and into the office where Karen was sitting across the desk from Captain Segura. "Ah, Señor!" Segura smiled and stood, and Karen rushed to examine Hartley's battered head even before the guards had moved away.

"I am so grateful that Mrs. Kellner spoke up," Segura said. "I hope you can find it in your heart to forgive this dreadful mistake."

"Your men play very rough," Hartley said. He held up his bloodstained fingers and pointed to the side of his head.

"He's had a bad blow," Karen said.

"Por Dios! Sergeant, get us a medic to treat this man," Segura said. The sergeant saluted and vanished, and Segura switched back to English, his smile again intact as he pointed to a chair. "Please sit down, Mr. Hartley. And let me apologize again for my men. They get excited."

"They can kill somebody."

"I'm sorry," Karen said. "I got you into all this."

"My men are only country boys, and some are very timid," Segura said.

"Timid!"

"Sometimes they overreact to the slightest questioning of their authority."

"I'm sure Colonel Negroponte will be glad to know about your problem with discipline," Hartley said.

Segura's amused smile wilted fully for the first time. "You know Colonel Negroponte?"

"I had dinner with him last night, and I will see him tomorrow morning."

"May I see your passport, Mr. Hartley?" Segura was dead serious now as Hartley dropped his passport beside Karen's on the desk. At his back, a soldier entered carrying a medical bag. "Treat Mr. Hartley's wound there," Segura said. He pointed to the place, and the medic began immediately, loosening Hartley's shirt and filling the room with the smell of disinfectant as he wet a cloth and began cleansing the side of Hartley's head and neck.

Segura closed the passport and looked across his desk. "Mrs. Kellner tells me you were her companion at the theater."

"I don't see that my reason for being at the theater is any of your business at all," Hartley said. And then he said, "Ouch!" as the disinfectant soaked stingingly into the cut on his head.

Segura smiled and for a moment looked off toward the wall. "Mr. Hartley, please try to understand. I've already explained to Mrs. Kellner. It is not that I wish to pry into the private lives of American citizens. But I need to know what they are likely to be doing in Nicaragua, if we are to avoid mistakes like this in the future. Why did you attend this abominable piece of theater?"

"You know very well the American view toward freedom of speech—freedom to consider new ideas," Karen said.

"Señorita, please. Yes. We in Nicaragua admire your Constitution. I hope one day we may have one like it. But even in your country, freedom of speech does not include the freedom to incite mobs to riot—which this play clearly did."

"It was an audience cheering in a closed building!" Hartley said.

"How long have you been in this country, Mr. Hartley?"

"Only a couple of days this trip. I lived here once as a child."

"Ah, then you probably are not yet fully aware of the dangers...."

"What dangers?"

"An active revolutionary force at work to overthrow our government, to stifle commerce, to destroy the church—in short, to completely...."

"So that gives *you* the right to arrest law abiding citizens?"

"Mr. Hartley, please...."

"...Anybody who doesn't think like you?"

"I understand you are angry. I, too, am angry that you were struck."

"I want that man's ass, Captain."

"Believe me, I will reprimand him myself." Segura looked up at the medic attending Hartley's cut. "Are you finished?"

"Sí. Es todo lo que puedo hacer." The medic backed out and through the door.

"It's all he can do," Segura said.

"May we go now, Captain?" Karen said.

"Yes, of course. But please, one moment. In spite of the way we have offended you—will you be good enough to let me explain?"

"Explain what?" Hartley said. "What's left?"

Segura shuffled their passports like playing cards. "That play was revolutionary, was it not?"

"Yes."

"It advocated the violent overthrow of the government—the violation of law. It even insulted your United States."

"Yes. It certainly did that."

"Now, try to put yourself in my place, Mr. Hartley. Tomorrow, when you talk to Colonel Negroponte, remember that this was no ordinary theater audience. I know these people. I know their reputations, their prison records. Some I have arrested before. What should I do? They were being urged to march on the prison of *El Castillo* and force the release of prisoners. Should I let the riot form and then try to stop it in the streets amid burning cars and dead bodies? Or should I stop it before it gets started?"

"They had committed no crime," Hartley said.

"No. Not yet. But I knew what they would do. And in my training with Special Forces at Fort Bragg, they taught me that the good officer is one who solves problems before they start." He smiled.

"Unfortunately, you were in the middle of my solution."

"Along with a lot of other innocent people, I'll bet," Karen said.

"Innocent people have nothing to fear," Segura said. "We will screen them and release them just as we are releasing you."

"You'd better hurry or you're going to have some dead ones on your hands."

"Before the night is over," Segura said. He stood, flexing their passports in his fingers as he came around the desk. "But please remember as you think about this in relation to your own Bill of Rights—your freedom of speech and freedom of assembly...." He handed back the passports. "A man may only be expressing his freedom when he strikes a match, but if he insists on doing it near a dangerous gasoline spill, I'm sure your authorities would stop him before he killed people. Tonight, I was merely trying to prevent a conflagration."

"You are very eloquent in your own defense," Karen said.

"I do my duty, Señora. And now, I will provide you with transportation back to your quarters."

Karen dropped her passport into her purse as Segura called his lieutenant from the next office. And then, as Segura came back into the room, Karen stopped him in the doorway. "Captain Segura, where is Tomás Rubio?"

"Rubio?"

"Was he arrested?" Segura breathed deeply as he studied her, and she repeated the question. "Was he arrested?"

"Yes."

"On what charge?"

"Señora, he wrote the play. He urged people to riot."

"You mean, he put his ideas on paper. What charge are you making?"

"Official charges have not been made, but I would say 'inciting to riot' or 'proposing to overthrow the government' or 'revolutionary activity.' Any one of them. Perhaps all of them."

"I want to talk with him," Karen said.

"Karen, you're crazy," Hartley said.

"Did you *like* his play, Señora?"

"How could I like his play? Rape, violence, attacking the U.S...? No, of course not. But I want to know why Rubio wrote this play."

"Señora, there are possibly other charges we could make against Tomás Rubio. We believe he is involved in subversive activities."

"He's the best known playwright in Latin America, Captain Segura, and I want to know why he hates us. All his other plays have been gentle—almost childlike. I'd like to explain the U.S. foreign policy to him."

"You've never met him, have you?"

"No."

"Well, I will tell you," Segura smiled. "I was in the same parochial school with Tomás Rubio. Arguing with him is not easy."

"Let me try. Maybe I can take him to the States and get him off your hands completely."

"Oh, Señora, it is like a comic opera."

"Look, Captain," Hartley said. "I don't know about Mrs. Kellner, but I would really like to get back to my hotel."

"Yes. Of course, Mr. Hartley. This has been a bad night for you."

"All right," Karen said. "All right. We'll go. But let me put it this way—as a representative of the U.S. government. We in the United States are interested in the career of Tomás Rubio. We have given aid and support to Nicaragua in the past, and I know that you would like for us to send additional military aid for the Guardia Nacional. But first, we would like to know that Nicaragua observes the same democratic freedoms we value—freedom of speech, freedom of the press, all the others. I'm sure the ambassador will be very upset if he hears how your men attacked Mr. Hartley and arrested me—a U.S. diplomat—along with a playwright, for exercising his God-given right of free speech. And I think you are going to have a nice international incident on your hands."

"Por Dios, Señora! You paint a very dark picture for me."

Karen was standing defiantly behind her chair and, in spite of his anger at her and the throbbing pain in his head, Hartley could not help admiring her as she turned part way toward the door and then looked back at Segura. "On the other hand," she said, "if you will release Tomás Rubio and arrange for me to talk with him at the embassy tomorrow, I may not have to report this incident to Ambassador Grubbs at all."

Segura breathed heavily and then turned slowly to Hartley. "And you, Señor—in your talk with Colonel Negroponte...?"

"I make no promises," Hartley said. "I'm not bound by her rules."

"No, of course not. But, will you at least consider...?"

"Perhaps," Hartley said. "For the embassy, perhaps. But I make no promises. Now just get us out of here."

"Yes. All right. Right away," Segura said. He turned to Karen. "It is probably a mistake, but I'll do it," he said. "I'll do what you ask. I'll release Rubio and take him to the embassy tomorrow."

"Good. I'm delighted," Karen said. "And you might also make sure he knows he's been released by U.S. influence. I want him to love us."

"It is all so mixed," Segura said.

"Can we go now, Captain?"

"Yes, yes. Of course." Segura motioned toward the door. "My lieutenant will take you in my own car while I remain here and make sure that justice is done."

"Tomorrow morning," Karen said. "In my office. Eleven o'clock."

And then they were riding in the back seat of an army sedan and curving through the streets. "I'm sorry," Karen said as they came down the mountain. "I had no idea there was any danger tonight."

Hartley nodded, but his eyes were burning and, almost against his will, he closed them.

"How's your head?"

"It hurts."

"That Captain Segura!" Karen said. "He reminds of a panther."

"A panther?"

"Doesn't he you?"

"You've seen too many movies."

"No. Really. Can't you see him—like a caged animal. Moving, calculating, dangerous...."

"You seem to have pulled his claws tonight."

"I wouldn't trust him for anything you could name." They were at her apartment now, and the air was filled with the odor of night-blooming jasmine. "You want to come in for some aspirin or something?"

"I have some at the room," Hartley said. "I think I'd better go on."

She opened the door and looked back. "Believe me, I'm sorry," she said again. "I hope you won't write me off as a total loss."

"You were rather magnificent, if you want to know the truth," Hartley said.

"What?"

In spite of the pain, he was able to smile. "I hate to admit it, but you handle yourself well under fire."

"Oh," she said. "Thank you for saying that." She looked suddenly very girlish as she stepped out of the car. "Thank you a lot. I'll call tomorrow and see how you are."

She reached back and touched his hand on the seat, and then she was up the steps and through the door.

"Vamos," Hartley said to the driver. "Vamos."

14

From the small bedroom of his house, Jonathan Quetoda heard the pounding on the front door. Maria was at the rear of the house working to set up her infirmary, and for a long moment Quetoda just listened until the knocking came again, more insistently this time, and he hurried forward. When he opened the door, he found himself gazing squarely into the pale face of an officer of the Guardia Nacional.

"Pastor Jonathan Quetoda?" the officer said.

"Yes."

"I am Lieutenant Fazio."

"Oh," Quetoda said. And then, as he opened the door further, he gasped. Behind the lieutenant stood a sergeant with a rifle, and beside the sergeant, kneeling on the steps of the porch, were two campesinos with badly bruised faces. The air was rich with the smell of rum. "What is this?" Quetoda said, but Lieutenant Fazio ignored the question and acted as though the kneeling campesinos did not exist.

"I'm sorry we haven't met before," Fazio said.

"But..."

"Your predecessor, the American missionary, was so very prompt in visiting us during his first days in our province."

Somehow Quetoda felt compelled to look back into Fazio's eyes. "I have been very busy, calling on my congregation, settling my wife," he said.

"You have a wife?"

"Sí."

"I hadn't heard. I hope she'll like Baná. And we hope that you, and perhaps your wife, too, will come to visit us at Guardia headquarters one day. We depend so much upon our pastors and priests to help us maintain peace and order in our district."

"You do?"

"Yes, of course. But let's get on to the business of the evening. This is Sergeant Figuera." The sergeant braced, holding his M-16 tightly at port across his chest. "And I'm sure you know these worthless scum from your congregation." Fazio turned now as though giving permission with his eyes for Quetoda to look at the two men on the step.

Even in the dim light, Quetoda could see that their faces were caked with dried blood, and the combined smell of fresh rum and stale human sweat was overpowering as he knelt to look at their wounds. "Pablo," he said to the older man, "What happened?"

But Fazio interrupted. "*I* will tell you of their crimes," he said.

And Quetoda stood again to face him. "These men are respected members of our congregation."

"Then they need better Christian training," Fazio said.

"Let me take them inside."

"One moment."

"They're hard workers—family men—excellent farmers—the best...."

"Just so," Fazio said. "But when some people have excellent reputations, they tend to get above themselves. They want more than is their due. They harass their neighbors and their neighbors' wives."

"Can this be?"

"I assure you," Fazio said. He pointed contemptuously toward the kneeling men. "These men—in the Rameses bar in the town of Baná, drinking and carousing, bragging of their exploits and challenging other people."

"I cannot believe...."

"We hope for their rehabilitation in your hands, Pastor. Scare the 'bejesus' out of them, as my American instructor used to say, scare the 'bejesus' out of them. We hope that the power of your Protestant church will do for them what the *true* church and the laws of Nicaragua seem unable to achieve." Fazio stepped back beside his sergeant and gave a mock hand salute, smiling over his shoulder as he turned away. "But let me again invite you, as sincerely as I can, to visit us at headquarters one day soon."

The men kneeling on the steps seemed about to faint, and when the officer had gone, Quetoda took them inside to lie on the rug near the front while he ran to the rear of the house for Maria.

In a moment, she was with him, carrying the emergency kit with the few medicines and bandages she had brought from the seminary, and he watched as she knelt on the floor to examine the men, loving her lean fingers as she worked over the bruised faces. "You need stitches," she said to Pablo. "I will try to close the wound with tape, but you should see a doctor."

"And where will I find a doctor out here?" Pablo said. "Besides, I could not pay."

"Hold still," Maria said. "I'm just telling you what you need." She pressed her tan fingers against the bandage on Pablo's sun-blackened face. "Jonathan, hold this gauze while I wrap the tape."

The other man, Sixto, had a broken nose, and when Maria had done the best she could with stiff bandages, the two men sat back and leaned against the wall beside the door. "We are very grateful, Pastor," Pablo said, "but this will not be the end of trouble. We did not do the things the lieutenant said."

"Then why were you arrested?"

"Your guess is as good as mine. But we think it was because we applied for our portion of land under the land reform law."

"But that's perfectly legal."

"Some people don't like it," Sixto said.

"Who?"

Pablo shrugged. "The land owners, the corporations...."

Quetoda stood back beside the table. "What about the

drinking?"

"We had one drink," Sixto said, "at the end of the day, when we completed the papers. We went to the bar, and these men came in to accuse us. One said I insulted his wife. Impossible. He struck me and threw rum in my face and, a moment later, the Guardia came to beat us more." Sixto stood and, for a moment, braced himself with one hand against the wall. "It's getting dark," he said. "I must go home. But don't you worry, Pastor. We'll go back to them again. We'll go back and take every farmer in the valley. We'll get what is rightfully ours."

15

Segura's call reached Karen promptly at eleven o'clock the next morning, his dark Spanish voice more tense than she remembered it. "Señora, we have a problem."

"What's the matter?"

"Our friend Rubio refuses to go to the embassy. I think—even if I take him there to release him—he will walk away or at least make the whole business very awkward."

"Why?"

"He says it would be groveling."

"Groveling? To whom?"

"He's very proud. He refuses to bow to North American pressure—in any form."

"I'll bet he'd like to have some of our money."

"If he is approached the right way, perhaps. But Señora, please. There are other issues since last night—things I cannot discuss on the phone. If you could release me from my promise...."

Karen stopped him in mid-sentence. "Bring him to the Teatro Nacional," she said. "I'll meet you in the lobby. Tell him I'll do the groveling, if that's the way he wants to see it."

"But...."

"I'm counting on you, Captain. Thirty minutes."

When she looked up from the phone, Rick Adams was smiling at her from the doorway. "If you'd just consult some of your old friends, you might stay out of trouble," he said.

"So you heard about last night."

"I don't know whether you or Segura has got the biggest tiger by the tail."

"Do you know Segura?"

"It's my job to know things. And people, too." He came in and leaned across her desk. "Just listen to me, Karen, Segura is dangerous. And so is Tomás Rubio."

"In what way?"

"They deal in people's lives."

"I think I can take care of myself, Rick. And right now I've got an appointment."

"Listen to what I'm telling you," Rick said. She moved toward the door, but he reached out and held her arm. "Nobody knows it yet, but I think we're on the edge of a nice little revolution, and I think Rubio's involved. Let Segura keep him now he's got him."

"Does Washington know all this?"

"They know everything we know. But it's hard to report the invisible. My advice to you is to stay away from these guys."

"You'd like that, wouldn't you?"

"Hell, Karen, I just don't want the job of bringing your body back from the alley behind El Castillo prison."

She ran out then without waiting to hear more, just glancing at her watch and leaving Rick standing in the doorway as she rushed to her newly assigned car and drove alone through the city for the first time, feeling now fully independent as she twisted through the mercado along the Avenida 19 de Mayo. Maybe she should have asked Rick more questions before rushing out, she thought. But, in honesty, she had to remember that Rick was always seeing revolutions. He lived in a world of invisible disaster, somewhere close to the border of paranoia, and she had learned long before that she couldn't trust his views, even if there were dangers involved.

But when she walked into the lobby of the Teatro Nacional and saw Segura and Rubio standing there, the last thing she felt was danger. Segura was the ideal of a military officer, trimly starched but not gaudy, his aquiline face greeting her with a smile over the heads of everyone else in the room. And Rubio beside him, looking at her through steel-rimmed glasses, was thin, unshaven, and slightly stooped, almost fragile as he leaned on his cane. "Ah, Mrs. Kellner," Segura said, "we meet again." He extended his hand and only then did she notice the other Guardia soldiers in the lobby. "As you requested, I have brought my old friend from school, the famous playwright, Tomás Rubio."

Rubio nodded but did not offer his hand as he continued to lean on his cane.

"What's his status?" Karen said.

"Oh, free—free as the birds in the sky," Segura said. "Never should it be said that the government of Nicaragua would compromise an artist's freedom of speech."

She knew he was playing with her, but she tried not to let it show in her voice. "Then thank you, Captain," she said. "If you'll excuse us, I'd like to talk privately with Señor Rubio."

"Of course. But if I may, I, too, will remain in the area. I would like to speak to you after your interview."

"If there's time," Karen said.

Segura bowed from the waist, turned away briskly, and was joined by two subordinates as he strode out of the building, his heels loud against the marble floor.

"Why did you set up this charade?" Rubio said. His green eyes were almost yellow in their intensity. "I really have nothing to say to an agent of the United States."

"Let's sit in the café," Karen said.

She led the way into the lounge to sit at the small round table beneath the painting of the Annunciation near the casement window. "Here." She patted the seat beside her like a mother with a small child. "For your information, this American agent was arrested for attending your play last night."

"You? Segura didn't tell me that."

She smiled up at him. "I wanted to see your play, and I went to jail for it. Now I want to talk to the playwright."

He was still standing beside the table, but with her smile, he reached to his knee and unlocked something beneath the leg of his trousers in order to sit. "He told me only that he had been ordered to bring me to you for release."

"He doesn't want to tangle with the embassy," Karen said. "But, if it weren't for me, you'd still be in that jail cell."

"Don't you know he'll arrest me again as soon as you leave?"

"Not unless you commit some crime besides writing plays, he won't. I was quite clear with Captain Segura. We want our allies to observe the same democratic principles of free speech that we do in the U.S."

"Señora, really...."

Rubio smiled sardonically, but she went on without waiting. "Why did you write that play—*La Fuerza*, is that the title?"

"Because I decided to tell the truth."

"Were your other plays not true?"

"Oh yes, but...."

"I have to tell you, Mr. Rubio—or may I call you Tomás?"

"Yes, of course."

"Thank you. I'm Karen. And as cultural attaché at the U.S. Embassy, I think your other plays are beautiful. I think an American audience would love them, and I would...."

"Señora, I must insist!" He tapped with his cane against the floor like a judge calling for order. "The people of the United States are no more *American* than the people of Nicaragua or Costa Rica. Only more arrogant."

"What?"

"They have no more claim to the name *American* than we do."

"Oh...."

"North American, South American, Nicaraguan, Canadian. But please, don't give it all to the United States."

"I'm sorry."

"Let us be precise, if we are going to talk."

The voice from his slim body possessed great power, and she could feel her scalp tingle under his reproach. "It's a habit," she said.

"Yes. Well my job as a writer is to shake people out of their habits."

"You don't make conversation very easy, do you?"

"Why should I? If we have something important to say, we will say it. Otherwise, we can spare each other the small talk."

"For a man who spent the night in jail...."

"Is that why I'm here? To show gratitude for my release?"

"No, of course not."

"Because, if it is, I'm afraid my knees don't bend very well."

"*No*. I told you."

"Good. Now, what were you saying about my plays?"

For a moment, she had trouble refocusing. "You make things difficult for yourself, did you know that? I would like to see your folk plays produced in the States."

He looked at her without speaking.

"...As part of a cultural exchange," she said.

"No artist can be opposed to a wider audience."

"It could mean a great deal of money."

"Why do you say *only* the folk plays?"

"They show the people of this country in a warm and sympathetic way."

"Is that what you mean by cultural exchange...?"

"What?"

"Showing nations in a warm and sympathetic way? Lots of sheep and goats playing with cherubic children on a green hillside?"

"No. Not necessarily."

"I take it you don't like *La Fuerza*."

"No patriotic American could like *La Fuerza*."

His green eyes bored into her, almost dancing with cold humor. "Old habits die hard, don't they?"

She tried to ignore him. "My companion called it propaganda."

"All art is propaganda, Señora. It's just that the best art hides it."

"I found it offensive."

"Then, so be it. Except for the last act, the story was barely more than factual journalism."

"And I'll tell you something straight," Karen said. "I can get you and your folk plays into the United States, but if the State Department hears about *La Fuerza*, they'll never grant you a visa."

"Is that your country's definition of free speech?"

"What?" she said again.

And suddenly he was laughing across the table directly into her face. "You don't even see it, do you?"

"See what?"

"You come here all righteous about free speech. You even get me out of jail for the sake of free speech—and for that I thank you, really I do. But now you tell me that the United States will not accept me unless my speech is clean—unless I say the right things."

"Why should we invite you there to insult us?"

"Only because your speech is free and you are interested in truth." He laughed again. "No, Señora, no. It is all illusion. Don't you see? You think your government supports free speech, but it does not. You think your government does benign and generous things, but that is also an illusion—unless the benign things pay dividends to your government. You hate my play because I shattered your illusions."

"I don't accept a thing you're saying."

"Then prove me wrong. Put your free speech to the test and take the acting company of *La Fuerza* to the States."

"I happen to like *La Broma*, the play that's here at the Teatro Nacional. It's a better play."

"One can always find justifications, Señora, if you look hard enough."

"You're insufferable, you know that?"

He laughed again. "Let me tell you something." He leaned back to straighten his crippled leg, and a shadow of pain crossed his face as the metal brace clanked beneath the table. "Yes, there are cherubic babies in Nicaragua," he said, "and lambs and goats, too. That much is true. But, Señora, over half the babies of this country are sick with enteritis and filled with parasites. There are no schools except for the rich; there is no medical care in the provinces. Diphtheria and polio are still uncontrolled." He stood and lifted the leg of his trousers to show his withered calf supported on both sides by steel braces which fitted into special high top shoes. "Yes. Polio!" he said. "And I'm one of the lucky ones. I was born into the privileged classes. *I* received care. In the provinces, if I had lived at all, I would be crawling like an animal for the rest of my life."

He sat back quietly for a moment, but Karen could see that everyone in the café had turned to look at them. "Ah," Rubio said. He waved toward the Guardia soldier who was watching from the corner. "Sometimes I get excited. But if you want art that depicts the character of the nation, don't ask me to write only about cherubic babies and fleecy lambs."

"How can all this be true?" Karen said. "Statistics show economic growth at about ten percent. How can...?"

"Statistics never tell who gets the money, Señora. But I will tell you. It goes to President Somoza and his family, to his friends and his supporters. It goes to the politicians and the military. And it also goes to the U.S. corporations that do business here without paying taxes. Virtually nothing goes to social service. And precious little to the workers who make it all possible."

"But we provide loans—aid for health and education."

"So model schools and hospitals are built for the wealthy."

"I don't believe it," she said. "I just don't believe it."

"And you have also sent military aid. Don't forget that. Until two years ago, you sent arms and trained Somoza's army for him. Your country created the Seguras of Nicaragua who are so beautifully efficient." He leaned back and smiled again. "So now when I depict a Guardia soldier in the act of rape, I put a U.S. flag on his back."

"Have you eaten lunch?" Karen said.

"Señora, I have spent the night in jail. I've had nothing but a swallow of water since yesterday."

"Then let's...."

He touched her arm, and his green eyes took in the entire room without his once turning his head. "Will you help me escape?"

"I've been trying to offer you a trip to the States, if you'll cooperate."

"No, I mean now—today."

"But you're free."

"I told you—as soon as you're gone, they'll arrest me again. And I have to tell you—completely aside from the free speech issue, which is only an issue because they arrested you by mistake, they have been trying to arrest me for a long time."

"Why?"

"I have advocated revolution, the overthrow of the government."

"But only in your writing, one of your characters...."

"It's enough for a firing squad, believe me." He leaned toward her. "I've unmasked them. The government had been making gestures of greater freedom—more openness, the promise of land reform, even allowing some unions to exist. But *La Fuerza* was a test. I've revealed their hypocrisy. Their promise of greater freedom is just another sham. Nothing has changed and I need your help."

"Let's walk across to the hotel dining room," Karen said. She gathered her purse, and Rubio clanked the metal brace at his knee as he followed her out beneath the gilded ceiling of the lobby and past the three Guardia soldiers who watched them and then followed at a distance as they walked slowly down the steps into the sunshine. "Although you sound plausible, I don't necessarily believe anything you've told me," Karen said. "And I have to tell you: officially—beyond my concern for your plays and the business of cultural exchange—I am a representative of the United States, and the United States supports the government of Nicaragua. Their enemies are our enemies. You have to understand that."

"I never doubted it."

"Reform the government through peaceful debate if you can. But if you or anyone else tries to overthrow it with arms, we in the States will do everything necessary to crush you. Now then...." They were beneath the purple flowers of the venenera vine as they approached the arches of the old hotel. "...Aside from that, there may be something else we might try."

Hartley had returned from his meeting with Cortez and the

officers of Agri-21, and he had just finished talking to Brad about the completed deal, when the phone rang immediately again, and he recognized Karen's voice even before she told him who it was.

"How's your head?" she said.

"Oh, much better, thanks. Sore, but O.K. How're you?"

"Fine, and I'm downstairs in the lobby—with a friend. Can we come up?"

"Yes. Of course."

He slipped the newly signed loan contract for Agri-21 into his briefcase: one million, two hundred thousand dollars at 16 percent. It was a sweet deal for the bank, and it had been his responsibility almost from the beginning. The money wouldn't even have to change hands. The bank would just deposit it into the defaulted loan account of Walter Guy's Ajax Equipment Company, Walter Guy would ship the tractors to Agri-21 in Nicaragua, and First International Bank would again have a performing loan invested with reliable clients. It should be worth a good bonus at the end of the year, he thought. And even though his neck was stiff from the events of the previous night, Hartley was whistling to himself when the knock came and he walked across the room to open the door.

"Surprise!" Karen said. "This is Tomás Rubio."

"Rubio?" Hartley said. And then he recognized the name. "Now, wait a minute! You're the guy who caused all the trouble last night!"

"Ron, he was arrested with us!"

"Well, I don't remember him getting the butt of a carbine up against the side of his head the way I did. And believe me...," he pointed at Rubio, "...*you're* the one who deserves it."

"I guess we came to the wrong place," Karen said.

"Wrong place for what? Somehow I thought you'd come to inquire about my health."

"I did. But...." She was almost as tall as he, and she looked directly into his eyes. "How would you like to get back at the men who arrested you last night?"

"Karen, what are you talking about?"

"If you'd calm down a little, we might be able to tell you. Can we come in?"

Hartley looked again at Rubio, sighed and backed away from the door. "Yes. All right."

"Let me look at your head."

"Karen...."

"No. Turn around." He did as she told him, and her hands were cool against the back of his neck. "Is your headache gone?"

"Yes."

"Good. You see, Tomás. The only person injured in the arrest last night was an innocent American."

"I'm sure that would not hold true by this morning," Rubio said. "But in any case, Mr. Hartley, I am sorry you were injured while attending my play."

"I hope you'll write a better one next time."

"I'm trying to convince Tomás that all Americans are not children of the Great Satan," Karen said.

"Oh, Señora, I do not believe all North Americans are evil. They are merely innocent and uninformed, fallen among bad companions."

"He is also an arrogant and patronizing bastard," Hartley said.

"Yes. And to that you can add *stubborn*," Karen said. "But Ron, he needs help."

Captain Segura was waiting in the lobby when Karen and Hartley came downstairs a few minutes later. They had walked down the steps to avoid the elevator man, but as they rounded the corner of the stairwell, Segura was standing at the front desk, blocking the way. "Ah, Señora, I was afraid I had missed you," he said. "And Señor, how is your health today?"

"Much better," Hartley said. "Colonel Negroponte was very solicitous this morning."

Segura's smile vanished for just an instant. "Que será, será," he said. "I was hoping you might forgive us more fully." He turned to Karen. "Where is Tomás Rubio?"

"He left."

His smile was gone completely. "How? When?"

"It was strange," Karen said. "We had lunch and he went to the men's room. He never came back."

Segura turned away and spoke to a Guardia lieutenant who hurried off in the direction of the men's room. "Can we talk now?" he said as he turned back.

"I'm afraid not now," she said. "I have many things to do at the embassy."

"Perhaps I could ride with you. We could talk in the car."

"Mr. Hartley is coming with me," Karen said. She took Hartley's arm and pushed him gently toward the door. "But if you'd call my secretary and make an appointment, I'm sure we could find a convenient time."

She propelled Hartley forward, and it was only when they were seated in the car that she spoke again. "I hope you don't mind."

"Kidnapping and arrest seem to be a way of life here," Hartley said.

"I really appreciate your coming. I would just as soon keep Segura at a safe distance."

"You're a dangerous woman, did you know that?"

"Me?"

"And a very persuasive one, too. You may have just talked me into sheltering a hard line Marxist revolutionary in my hotel room."

"God! I hope not. I was thinking of him only as a writer. You have to trust something in this world, don't you?" She glanced at him but he didn't reply. "Don't you?"

"A man with a crippled leg is certainly worthy of your compassion," Hartley said.

"You don't sound very convinced." She looked back at the street. "But anyway, as a reward for your cooperation, you are hereby invited to every event connected with the coming U.S. symphony concert."

"The symphony concert?"

"Yes. It's the first project Ambassador Grubbs gave me. You

know, trying to improve international relations through the arts. So you're invited."

"Well...."

"With me...."

"Oh."

"...If you think you could take it."

"O.K." Hartley said. "Yes. Fine. Nothing ventured, nothing gained, I suppose. But Karen, believe me. This time, I'm gonna be ready to duck a lot quicker."

16

It was late in the afternoon when Quetoda learned from Maria that the men had gone en masse to make their complaint to the government land office. Maria had seen Pablo's wife in the market. "They didn't even bother to stop in Baná," Maria said. "They went all the way to the capital, to the minister of agriculture."

"How many?"

"Twenty or thirty, I think. On the little bus."

"I hope they have no trouble," Quetoda said.

But even as he said it, he felt better that the men had not gone back to the office in Baná—and relieved that they had gone without him. Certainly the people at the head of government should be more sympathetic, he thought. Still, when night came, he felt anxious and uneasy. On the one hand, he was disappointed with himself for feeling so relieved that the men had not asked him to go with them; on the other, he felt a concern for their safety. For a long time, he lay listening in the dark to the relaxed and heavy breathing of Maria at his side, and then just as he was about to drift off to sleep, he heard a sudden and powerful knocking on the door of his house.

Maria jumped from her sleep in an instant and was clutching his arm against her bare breast. "What is it?" she said. But now they could both hear the voices of women, high and on the edge of panic, "Pastor! Pastor! Help us!" And in a moment, both he and Maria were at the door, Maria now in a loose smock and he wearing only his trousers and no shoes as he slipped the bolt and the two women burst through, weeping and crying, "Pastor, they killed them!" It was Blanca, Pablo's wife, and Iris, the wife of Sixto, Blanca approaching him directly, almost as an assault and pounding his bare chest. "They are dead! They are dead and lying in the field!"

"Who is dead, Blanca? Where?"

"Pablo. Pablo is dead. And Sixto!"

"When? How?"

"The men came back from Managua, but Pablo and Sixto did not come home from the bus. We were waiting till late, and then we heard this car and someone shouting, 'Come and get your men, come and get your men. We've brought back your troublemakers!' In the car light, we could see them dragging bodies to the field."

"Take us to them," Maria said. "Maybe they're still alive."

"Yes," Quetoda said. "Let me get a lantern and my shoes." And then they were off into the night with only the sounds of frogs and crickets beside the dusty road and the quiet keening of the women as Maria tried to comfort them.

When his lamplight found the two bodies lying face down in the tall weeds, his hand was shaking so that the light danced unsteadily and, for a moment, he was unable to move forward another step. But Maria didn't hang back. "Come," she said. "Put down the light and help me turn them over." And suddenly she was leading the way.

A strong chemical scent rose in the still air as they struggled to turn the bodies on the uneven ground. And Maria began groping in the dark for a wrist, feeling for a pulse even before he raised the light again. But this time, when the light fell on the men, even Maria dropped the wrist and jerked backward. "God! What animals!" And the two wives behind him screamed in a high wail of sheer terror at the sight of the dead men's jellied faces which had been liberally doused with acid. For a moment, he thought he was going to vomit, gagging and heaving twice and looking away until he could control himself. When he looked back, Maria was again examining the bodies, checking for any sign of life before she stood in finality beside them. "Acid and bullets," she said. "This was on Pablo's shirt." She was holding a paper in her hand, and she unfolded it in the light. "Death to all communists," the note said. "Anyone who buries these men will show us who our enemies are."

"We have to take them in," Blanca said, "into the house or the church."

"The police," Quetoda said. "The Guardia must see them before they're moved."

"But we can't leave them here!"

"It's almost dawn," he said. "Almost day. I'll go to the police— bring them as soon as I can. Stay with these women." He placed the lamp in Maria's hand and started off through the darkness toward his own house. "But Maria...." He stopped and called back to her from the edge of the field, "Don't move those bodies again— for any reason."

He was waiting on the steps of Guardia headquarters when Lieutenant Fazio arrived, riding behind his driver in the rear seat of an open jeep, and jumping out as he saw Quetoda. "Well, Pastor, what brings you to our headquarters so early?" He was smiling and swishing a swagger stick, but his playful mood changed quickly when he heard of the dead men. "Bring two men and come with me!" he said to Sergeant Figuera on the steps. And, within minutes, they were riding back along the dusty road the way Quetoda had come before dawn.

There were photographs, of course, the lieutenant himself taking the camera from Sergeant Figuera and snapping the angles, all the while talking, questioning the two widows between shots as the sun broke clear above the trees. "Señora, tell me once again the time."

"After midnight," Blanca said.

"Precisely, please."

"I don't know. Maybe one o'clock."

"Hmmn. And the car? What kind of car?"

"I don't know one car from another."

"Like my jeep?"

"No. Closed. A high back, like a truck. Very new."

Lieutenant Fazio knelt and looked again carefully at the bodies in the morning sun. "Killed by pistol at close range," he said. "The powder burns are clearly visible." He folded the note that had been pinned to the body of Pablo and slipped it into his breast pocket as he stood. "Señoras, permit me to offer you my deepest feelings of regret. I shall do my best to find the killers." He turned and gestured to Figuera, and the men moved ahead of him toward the jeep.

"Wait, Lieutenant," Quetoda said. "We will need your help. That note—the burial...."

"Burial of the dead is not the responsibility of the Guardia," Fazio said.

"But...."

Fazio smiled as he took his seat beside the driver. "Let me know if you have any difficulties, Pastor."

A shadow moved silently across his face as the jeep drove away, and Quetoda looked up to see a vulture gliding by at treetop level. Soon there would be others, he thought. He could hear the women talking at his back, and now that the Guardia was gone, people from the countryside were coming to gawk and make faces of disgust over the bodies. "We will make a stretcher and take them to the churchyard," the women were saying.

But Quetoda stopped them. "Wait," he said.

"Why?" Maria said. "They must be buried immediately."

"Come here." He gathered them close beside him in the shade and spoke as quietly as he could. "Which of these people looking on is a friend?" he said. "Pull them into the shade and keep the birds away. When the men come from the fields, I'll find someone with tools to help me."

At sundown, he found the men at the crossroads half a mile

from the church, the men coming in twos and threes along the dusty road with their machetes swinging from their sides, and he singled out the ones he knew. "I have to see you. There has been a catastrophe."

They followed him into the shade outside the church where they squatted on the ground or leaned against the building as he talked. "Pablo and Sixto must be buried," he said. "I need your help."

A long moment passed before anyone moved or spoke.

"Do you know who did it?"

"No. But I have to tell you—there was a note...."

"What kind of note?"

He told them, quoting the note as closely as he could, and again there was no response until two men rose silently from the edge of the group, dusted themselves off and moved away. "Wait," Quetoda said. "Who's going to help?"

"Pastor, there is no help."

"But we must give our friends a Christian burial."

"Those bodies are not our friends," the man said. He was a small man with a hoe across his shoulder. "Our friends are dead. There's nothing we can do."

"But...."

"If we bury them, we'll be marked, Pastor. They'll kill us too, and I'm not willing to die for a dead man." Others were rising, drifting away.

"It's your duty...."

"*Your* duty, maybe. We have better things to do." There were now only four men left standing beside the church. "If I risk my life, it will be for the living," the small man said.

And then there was only one man, a large Indian named Gaspar whom he had seen at one of the earlier meetings. "Will you help?" Quetoda said.

Gaspar gave a kind of shrug, a slight movement of his head and shoulders. "Well, Pastor, I am no more eager to risk my life than the others. But the body is all we have, no? Tonight we can do it in darkness."

"You're a true Christian."

"No, Pastor." Gaspar smiled slowly. "I am not a believer at all. But when I die, I hope someone will bury me."

And together, they buried Pablo and Sixto in the corner of the churchyard, digging, shoveling, picking through the stony soil, preparing the two graves far into the night and summoning the women for the final service by flickering lamplight. "Ashes to ashes, dust to dust.... The Lord giveth and the Lord taketh away.... In my Father's house are many mansions.... Believe on me and thou shalt be saved...." Quetoda sought in the darkness for the passages of consolation. And afterward, after the final prayer, as Maria escorted the two widows back to their houses, he and Gaspar refilled the graves.

When it was over, he washed beneath the single faucet of the outdoor shower and dropped his clothes on the porch as he came naked into the darkened house. Even without the light, he knew from the tension in the room that Maria was not in the bed, and after a moment he found her silhouette at the window against the night sky.

"Are you all right?" she said.

"Yes. Tired."

And then she came across the room, suddenly clutching him in the darkness, "Jonathan, I'm so afraid!"

"Yes."

She too was naked, and she crushed her body into his, seeking sanctuary, pressing flesh against flesh, bone against bone. "What does it mean? What does it mean? Will someone harm you for burying those men?"

"I don't know."

They lay on the hard bed still clutching each other. But in spite of his weariness, Quetoda felt that he would never sleep again. He had wanted to keep his church out of politics, but there was no way now that he could do it, no way now to keep himself or Maria out of danger. Merely performing or not performing his pastoral duties would be taking a stand, would make him someone's enemy.

Eventually, on his shoulder, Maria drifted off, but he lay there wide-eyed, reliving every experience of the day, echoing in his mind the words and screams of the women, the words of the Guardia officer, the words of the men coming home from the fields, and finally the sound of his own voice as he quoted the scriptural passages to the widows, "The Lord giveth and the Lord taketh away...," " "...In my Father's house...," " "...Believe on me...," all the while seeking some other passage that might serve as a guide for himself, something that would help him calm the anguish in his heart, until as Maria's breathing deepened, he remembered a troubling passage from St. Matthew: "I come not to bring peace but a sword..., to set a man at variance against his father and the daughter against her mother..., and a man's foes shall be they of his own household.... He that findeth his life shall lose it and he that loseth his life for my sake shall find it...."

What does it mean? Quetoda thought. He shivered in the tropic night as he thought of the soft sound of earth falling on human faces in the grave, and he clutched Maria ever closer against his heart.

17

Karen worked through the afternoon making calls, writing notes, and checking accommodations for the symphony musicians. The whole business was an inherited project, and it had been waiting for her when she first walked in to meet the ambassador. "The big thing coming down the pike for you right now is the United States Symphony," Ambassador Grubbs had told her. She remembered that it was the third sentence he spoke—even before "How are you?" and "Did you have a good trip?" He just said, "Hello, Miz Kellner. Have a seat." And then he walked back around his desk to pick up the half-burned cigar from his ash tray and started talking. "The big thing coming down the pike...." He spoke through blue smoke, with the tones of South Carolina ringing clearly as he relit the cigar. "Now, mind you, it wasn't my idea," he said. "It was the State Department and your predecessor, Peter Swineford. But since it's coming, I want to have a gala night," he said, "invite President Somoza and all the ministers of government, invite all the military leaders—and their wives, of course. Invite all the Americans who're here—at least the big people, the corporation people, you know, especially like the Kingstons at American Fruit Company. You think you can do that?"

"Sounds like a great idea," Karen said.

"I mean, I didn't really order this symphony, but since it's coming, we may as well make the most of it."

"It's wonderful," Karen said. "I'm sure we can do it." And from that point, she and Ambassador Grubbs had gotten along famously. He'd seen that she had a good office and that her apartment was comfortably furnished, and she had started work with enthusiasm. But now, although she knew she was making progress in preparing for the arrival of the symphony, she periodically caught herself staring off into the distance as events of the previous twenty-four hours overwhelmed her: the arrest..., the courtyard of El Castillo Prison..., Rubio..., the cut on Hartley's head. And Segura.

What was it she had said to Hartley? That Segura reminded her of a panther? Surely, at El Castillo, he had been the human personification of primitive and efficient brutality. And certainly she despised his macho tyranny when he strutted with his swagger stick. But then, standing beside Rubio in the lobby of the Teatro Nacional, Segura had been as suave as a Spanish David Niven, infinitely more polished and cosmopolitan than her own boss, Ambassador Grubbs, would ever be. What was he, really? she wondered.

And then her secretary looked in from the outer office and brought her suddenly back to the job at hand. "Mrs. Kingston is on line one."

"Oh, wonderful."

And the voice of Amanda Kingston came to her from another world, the cultured and ebullient Southern voice long accustomed to unquestioned command, almost singing to her over the telephone. "Yes, my dear, I'm so delighted you want to include us in the affairs of the embassy. We became very close to your predecessor, Mr. Swineford and, of course, to Ambassador and Mrs. Grubbs while Mr. Swineford was there, and I'm really thrilled that you're going to continue his cultural policies."

"And maybe do even more," Karen said.

"Splendid! It means so much to us Americans to know that the embassy is consciously concerned about us."

"The Kingstons and the American Fruit Company are one of our main concerns," Karen said.

"You're very kind, my dear, and very flattering. And of course, I don't believe a word of it," Amanda Kingston said, laughing. And then she got down to business. Certainly, she and Philip Kingston wanted to entertain the symphony, yes, even host a reception, a *soiree*, she called it. "It happens all too rarely," she said. "And there's really nothing Philip and I enjoy more than entertaining the diplomatic community and figures from the arts. It's really the American ideal, isn't it? The mixing together of nations and cultures?"

"I feel that way, too," Karen said.

"Mr. Swineford was nice, of course, but it's so good to have an intelligent woman in the job. I'll call you soon—in a day or so—to meet you personally."

"I would like that," Karen said. "Yes. I'll look forward to it."

The jasmine was just opening as she reached her apartment at sundown, and she breathed deeply, feeling now that the odor meant *home*. Wonderful, she said to herself. She reached into her purse for her keys and then, just as she was about to open the door, she heard a sound and jumped with surprise as she turned to find Captain Segura standing by the flower-covered lamp post.

"Forgive me, Señora, if I startled you."

"No, it's all right. I thought I was alone." Her heart was suddenly pounding, and she gripped the door key between her fingers without inserting it into the lock. "What can I do for you?"

"Well...," He looked down at the key. "I would like to apologize once again for any inconvenience that I may have caused you last night." He had slipped into Spanish, using the soft subjunctive— *quisiera*—and the clear, almost Castilian pronunciation of the educated classes.

"I understand, Captain."

"I suppose a mass arrest is not a good procedure," he said. "Next time, I will be more careful. But frankly, I was enraged. Both the Guardia and the United States had been maligned."

"Yes."

"I should have been more restrained, but...," He shrugged. "In any case, I want to thank you for understanding my position."

She looked at him standing there below her on the doorstep in the dusk, now without his swagger stick or his pistol, and she knew what he must have looked like as a little boy gazing up at his mother. The keys rattled in her fingers. "Why don't you come in for a minute," she said, "perhaps have a cup of coffee...."

"Oh, Señora...."

"Or maybe I've got some sherry."

"You are very kind."

He followed her inside and watched as she rummaged through a partially unpacked box of her recently arrived belongings. After a moment, she found the sherry and held the bottle up for his approval. "Some of this?"

"Excellent," he said. "Yes."

"I never thought I'd be having sherry with the policeman who arrested me."

"Oh please, I wish you would not think of me as a policeman," he said. "It's what I do at present. But really, I am an officer in the army of Nicaragua. This police work is just a necessary part of Guardia intelligence."

She sat beside him on the sofa. "Why did you go into the Guardia at all?"

"What other career is open to a fourth son in Nicaragua?" he said.

"Fourth son?"

"Yes. And my brothers much older than I. You might say I was my mother's last surprise." He laughed and lifted his glass, "To you, Señora. I pledge the Guardia to your service. May your stay in Nicaragua be long and happy."

With the taste of sherry, she was again aware of the scent of jasmine that had drifted to her on the warm air through the open door. "Thank you," she said.

"Besides, in Nicaragua, the military leads to everything else," Segura continued. "Oh, there was the priesthood, yes, but I am not—how would you say?—of a priestly disposition. And business—but I find that business bores me beyond belief, always the preoccupation with trading products, counting the cost or adding up the gain. And anyway, my mother was a widow, so, by the time I was ready for school, the military was the only way open. But I have to admit that my ultimate goal is the diplomatic service."

"Oh."

"The opportunity to promote the best of my nation."

"I see," Karen said. But even as she spoke, she realized that for several minutes she had not heard a single word he had said. She had been listening only to the hypnotic and liquid sound of his voice, the tone reaching her almost like a song as he spoke from the opposite end of the sofa.

"But I did not come to talk about myself," he said abruptly. "There is something else." He drained his glass and stood looking down at her. "Although I meant everything I said before, I must tell you that I am not really sorry about last night because last night I met you, and you are the most beautiful woman I have ever known...."

"What...!?"

She stammered a confused response, trying to stop him, but he didn't even hesitate. "...from the moment that you spoke out fearlessly at the prison, a woman undaunted, the most exquisite, somehow above all others...."

"Wait...!" She was almost shouting, but nothing she said seemed strong enough to interrupt the flow of his spoken song as he reached out and took her hand.

"...the most perfect woman I have ever seen, and I have fallen in love with you."

"What?! No. That can't be!" she said.

But without any hesitation at all, he pulled her to her feet and took her powerfully into his arms and kissed her, speaking now urgently, "I love you, Karen, I love you," and he reached down to cup her breast firmly in his hand.

"Captain Segura, wait, please."

"My name is Raúl."

"Please wait!" Her voice was shaking but she was able to place her palms flat against his chest, and now she could feel the energy surging like an electrical charge beneath his surface as she looked into his eyes. "Raúl, I am a widow," she said. And, almost instantly, he moved his hands and held her by the shoulders. "No habia tenido...." She tried to speak in Spanish, but in the torrent of confusion that engulfed her, the words would not come, and she continued in English. "I have been afraid of men. Since my husband died in the war. I have avoided men—avoided anything except business, or strict friendship." And then she lied, "You are the first even to kiss me." She did not like to lie, but he was like an unexploded bomb, and she was reaching for any shield she could find. There had been only Rick for that brief time in Washington, after all, and that was over. "You have moved me very deeply," she said. And that was not a lie. "You have moved me, very much, but..., we must wait...."

"Karen," he said, very softly, pronouncing her name with an elongated "a," *Kahren*, speaking tenderly and kissing her again, "Karen, Karen, how long, how long must we wait?" pressing her to him and wrapping her in his powerful embrace from toe to shoulder, until, like an exploding rocket, the sound of the telephone burst suddenly through the room.

"God!"

"Where is it?" Segura said. "I'll tear it off the wall!"

"No, Raúl, no. Wait." For a moment she had to think. In moving furniture, she had pushed the phone across the floor, somewhere behind the end table. Again it rang as she followed the sound.

"Must you answer it?"

"Yes. If I don't and it's the embassy.... Hello!" She bumped her head on the table just as she found the phone and answered. "Oh, God!" And instantly she recognized the voice of Ron Hartley.

"What's the matter?" he said.

"I couldn't find the phone."

"I was getting worried."

"I bumped my head."

"I'm sorry. Are you all right?"

"Yes, I think so. I'm O.K."

Segura pulled her to him as she talked and for a moment listened at the edge of the receiver.

"I thought you should know," Hartley said. "When I came in, my room had been ransacked and Rubio was gone."

"What? Was anything stolen?"

"No. But they dumped my briefcase on the bed and went through everything in the room, even my underwear. I had the hotel move me to another room with a chain on the door. I don't know what happened to Rubio."

"I guess there's nothing we can do," she said.

"Frankly, I think it's a police job. That guy Segura's capable of anything."

She managed to turn and look directly into Segura's eyes as she drove her elbow into his ribs, forcing him to back away. "Yes. I agree."

"But I thought you should know."

"Yes. Thanks. Call me if you hear anything more, or if you think of a way the embassy can help."

"O.K." Hartley said. "But check the locks on your doors tonight. And stay away from Segura, if you can."

"Yes. I will. Believe me. Thank you."

When she hung up, her hand was trembling, and Segura was staring at her from the window. "Mr. Hartley is out of luck," he said. "You are mine." He took the phone from her hand and lifted the point of her chin to look into her eyes. "If not today, then one day soon. I'm willing to wait. After all, I'm not a savage as your friend Hartley seems to think, and I did not break into his room. I respect you infinitely as the widow of a brother military officer. But Karen...," he pulled her closer and kissed her once again, this time on the forehead, "...if any other man should try to touch you, I will kill him. Do you hear me?" And without another word, he turned and walked out into the night.

18

Quetoda felt the pain of the burial for three days after the funeral. The blisters on his left palm burst and wet the bedclothes during the night, and although Maria covered them with bandages, the suppurating skin reminded him anew of the acid soaked faces of the dead men, and that memory, combined with the physical pain of his muscles and joints, almost paralyzed him.

He did not even go to his small office at the church until sundown the following day, and then the silence of the building was intolerable, and he escaped quickly out along the white path where he could stand beneath clear sky and hear the green parrots quarreling invisibly in the trees beyond the forest line. Tomorrow was Sunday and he had to prepare a sermon, but the thought of doing it seemed impossible. His congregation would be looking to him for guidance. Even Maria was looking to him for guidance, for words that would calm their fears. But there were no words. There was only the strangling egg of ice that seemed to be permanently fixed like a goiter beneath his larynx. If it were not for Maria, he would simply disappear into the jungle, he thought. He would avoid all public roads until he came to the next town where he could catch the little train operated by the fruit company and then leave the country altogether. To where, he didn't know and he wouldn't care. He didn't have what it took to be a minister of the Gospel, and he had to face it.

But then there *was* Maria.

Maria.

And once again, with renewed resolve, he approached his office, forcing himself with sheer willpower to walk down the path and through the door. And thinking of the wives and children who had been bereaved, he reached for the Bible and turned to the Book of Job: "Naked came I out of my mother's womb, and naked shall I return thither: The Lord hath given and the Lord hath taken away...." And further down, as he flipped the pages, "Man that is born of a woman is of few days and full of trouble," and "The tents of robbers prosper, and they that provoke God are secure...." And he knew that none of it would serve.

He began pacing across the floor and back to the desk. These members of his church were people who had suffered, he thought. They were frightened, and he wanted something to comfort them, but.... He struck his fist into the palm of his hand, and the sudden pain from the lacerated blisters radiated up his arm and filled his chest with a throbbing ache. He closed his eyes as the pain washed over him, and then he looked back at the text. Job had been angry when he spoke those words, he thought. "The tents of robbers prosper." Job had been railing against God for the loss of his property and the deaths of his children. "God destroyeth the perfect and the wicked," Job had said, "He will mock at the trial of the innocent." And then Quetoda knew for the first time what the new sensation in his chest really was.

He slammed his right fist down again, resoundingly this time against the center of his desk, but he knew now that what he really wanted was to slam his fist into the smiling face of Lieutenant Fazio or of some other Guardia officer. And before he realized what he was doing, he had turned and hurled the open Bible against the wall where it seemed to hang for a moment before fluttering to the floor like a bird with broken wings. "Oh God!" Quetoda shouted then, his voice deafeningly loud in the small room. "Oh God! Damn them!" It was a prayer pure and simple, shouted at the memory of Fazio's face, the cruel face above the battered campesinos on the church steps, the cynical face smiling at the two widows in the tropic sun. The Guardia had intimidated every man in the Baná valley, he thought. Every man. And they had run like rabbits when he tried to bury Pablo and Sixto. Every man. Except Gaspar, who was not even a Christian.

He heard a sound at his back, and he turned to see Maria standing in the doorway. "Are you all right?" she said. "Are you all right? I heard you shouting...."

"No," Quetoda said. "No! I'm not all right at all. I'm sick, sick at the killing, sick at the cowardice of campesinos."

"Jonathan...."

"Tomorrow I'm supposed to preach a sermon to comfort the bereaved. But I don't want to comfort the bereaved. I want to yell at them. I want to shake them! I want to rail against everybody in the valley!"

"Jonathan, you can't!"

"Just let me write my sermon."

When she was gone, he picked up the Bible from behind the door and saw that its spine had been broken. But this time, turning the oddly fluttering pages, he found his text in the Book of James: "What doth it profit, my brethren, if a man say he hath faith, but have not works? ...If a brother or sister be naked and in lack of food..., and yet ye give them not the things needful to the body, what doth it profit? Faith, if you have not works, is dead in itself."

And so, he prepared. But on Sunday morning, instead of feeling relief, he felt more frightened than he had ever felt before. In spite of his desire to strengthen and inspire resolution in his congregation, the perverse Biblical passages buzzed through his head like hornets:

"God destroyeth the perfect and the wicked."

"The tents of robbers prosper."

"I come not to bring peace but a sword."

If God was capable of mocking the innocent and rewarding the wicked even as He clothed the lilies of the field, then God was totally unknowable, unreliable, and maybe even unlikable. And quite involuntarily he clamped one hand across his mouth. How could he even think such a thing? It wasn't that he didn't believe in God, no, of course not, but—but the idea wouldn't go away. The nature of God, as he now perceived it, was something totally unlovable. Frightening, yes. Awe inspiring, maybe. But not lovable. And not a source of comfort. Pablo and Sixto had turned the other cheek as they had been taught to do and for their efforts had received a face full of acid.

The bell was ringing now, no steeple chime but an ancient brass cow bell that one of the deacons sounded as a final summons to the faithful. And Quetoda inhaled deeply and moved to take his place behind the pulpit.

There was no organ or piano but a group of young people playing Indian flutes and drums to accompany the first hymn. He followed the established order of worship, relieved for a time to have something resembling a ritual—the confession, the Lord's Prayer, the Apostles' Creed. But then, as the time drew near for the pastoral prayer, the pressure of fear seemed nearly to burst his chest. He felt like an intruder. How could he, after his un-Christian and even blasphemous thoughts of the morning, dare to address God?

He solved the problem by praying mainly in behalf of the families and friends of Pablo and Sixto. And then, with virtually no time for transition, he launched directly into his sermon, speaking now without any form of piety or in softening phraseology: "My friends, in the week just past, every member of this congregation has been assaulted. We have been assaulted in the bodies of Pablo and Sixto. We don't know who killed them, but we do know that Pablo and Sixto had been working to improve the lives of every worker in the Baná valley. We know also that others have died in this same cruel way in the nation of Nicaragua." Already he could hear the anger in his voice, and he paused as his eyes swept the congregation. "Pablo and Sixto were working for you; they were working for me. And yet, in this congregation of their Christian brothers, not one man would come forward to give them an honorable burial! I will now read the New Testament text for today."

He opened the pulpit Bible and read the entire chapter of James, ending almost in a shout: "Faith, if you have not works, is dead in itself!"

And then he moved aside from the pulpit, departing almost completely from his prepared text: "When I first arrived in Baná, I was ignorant. I did not understand the cruel and crippling conditions under which the people of this province are forced to live. I believed that all injustice could be corrected by simply obeying the law and following the rules laid down by those in authority. But now I understand more. I understand that living a decent human life requires much more than passive obedience of the law by a few citizens. It requires that all of us work together for our common good.

"Pablo and Sixto worked for our common good, and we were glad to let them do it; Pablo and Sixto had faith, and we admired them for it; but when Pablo and Sixto died, their brothers deserted them. *You!*" he shouted. "*You* deserted them. *You* ran to your homes and locked your doors. What did you do there, pray? What are you doing here on Sunday morning—praying for a better life? What are you doing for the families of the dead men? Where are the works that illustrate your faith? What are you doing to make sure that the lives of those men are not wasted? Or are you denying them like Saint Peter, saying, 'I never knew them?'"

Quetoda now walked around in front of the pulpit, moving closer, holding his surprised audience spellbound as he leaned forward. "Well, let me tell you something, my friends: God works through human hands. You can pray all day, but if you sit on your hands, you sit on God's hands. The salvation of Jesus comes through sweat and blood and pain. Not through quietly withdrawing into your house.

"There was a note on the body of Pablo. It said, 'Death to all communists. Anyone who buries these men will show us who our enemies are.' Now, *I* am not a communist, but I say to you: the human body—made in the image of God—must be respected." Quetoda raised his hands and jerked aside the bandages as he held his lacerated palms toward the congregation. "And I will say to those who killed Pablo and Sixto that *I* buried those men. With the help of one other man, *I* buried them. I am not ashamed to be the enemy of murderers. And you, my brothers and my sisters, must make some decisions, too."

He was sweating heavily now, suddenly conscious of his own body for the first time since he began speaking. It was as though he had been caught in a flooding torrent and swept along until the river of his zeal had finally deposited him on this undefended island in front of his pulpit, and now waking from his trance, he knew that he had made himself totally vulnerable, totally exposed. He walked back behind the pulpit, and there waiting to jog him on was the text he had prepared.

"Now, I am not going to tell you what to do," he said. "Finally, that is your choice, depending upon the kind of world you choose for yourself and your children. If you find that the present conditions are adequate, then you have no need to try and change them. You will be entirely within the principles of Christianity if you meekly turn the other cheek when you are slapped by the policeman or when unknown men attack your wives and murder your brothers in the dark.

"But, if you are not satisfied with life as it is and you wish to change it, then, my brothers and sisters, life will become difficult indeed. Your present jobs will be at risk, your wages may be lost. Others of us also may die. And life for a time may become indescribably painful. But that also is the way of Christianity—to protect the little child, to gather alms for widows and orphans, to see the image of God in all men, and to bury the dead."

He went directly into the final prayer and the closing hymn, and when he walked away from the pulpit, he felt like a man drunk. Somehow, he made it to the front of the church to greet the members, who though they shook his hand, seemed reluctant and downcast like reprimanded children. And when finally, minutes later, he entered the parlor of their little house and saw Maria's back strangely stiff as she stood gazing through the window at the mountains in the midday sun, he felt that an unbridgeable gulf had opened between them. He removed his tie and unbuttoned his shirt, and still she neither turned nor spoke until he threw the tie across the back of a chair. And then her voice was quite small as she continued facing the window: "I am the most frightened woman in Baná."

Instantly, he felt the old goiter of ice at his throat. "Maria...?" He had watched her seeking life in the bodies of the mutilated men, had seen her comforting their widows, yet now she stood ramrod stiff, her normally soft shoulders squared defensively. "The most frightened woman!" she repeated.

"I spoke what was in my heart," he said.

"You spoke out your rage!" She turned now, moving toward him. "You spoke out your rage. You didn't preach the Gospel. You preached the anger of Jonathan Quetoda! You shamed your people. If they heard you at all, no man in that congregation can live with himself unless he risks his life to clear his record."

"I offered them nothing but pain and...."

"You made yourself a walking target. You made *me* a walking target. For those who oppose reform—you and I will be first on their list!"

And then suddenly, with one step, she was against him, embracing him, turning his face to hers and kissing him deeply, with a passion more sharp than anything he had known in their whole two years together, moving with such violence against his mouth that he could taste blood on his lip, "Por Dios! How I love you!" And a moment later they were naked on the bed of their tiny room, Maria still conducting him, urging him into her and coming twice in quick succession before he reached his climax. "Oh God, oh God, how I love you!" giving herself in a new and total way as though the danger and the possibility of instant death made everything between them infinitely more precious.

"Today," she said at length, "Today...," now lying back in his arms, tasting the salt of his skin as she spoke with her lip against his chest, "Today, everything is changed."

19

And Maria was right. It was hardly a day before the changes could be seen. Just until the men finished work on Monday and started drifting down the dusty road to the house. Quetoda could hear their heavy shoes on the porch as they came up the steps, coming singly or in pairs but coming this time without a clear leader, standing sheepishly downcast until Quetoda went out to meet them and Maria brought them a pitcher of cold water.

For a moment he stood there in the fading sunlight, glancing about, hoping to find Gaspar among them. But Gaspar did not appear, and as the men continued to assemble in the dusk, Quetoda pointed down the white path toward the church. "Let's go into the sanctuary," he said.

He led the way and, there in the yellow light, it was a small wiry man, Rodrigo Soleras, a deacon, who seemed to summarize the position of the men: "You have shamed us, Pastor."

Quetoda could only look down at the floor, unable to avoid embarrassment.

"You have shamed us," Rodrigo said, "but you told the truth. You're a very brave man and we need your help."

He listened, neither agreeing nor disagreeing, slowly tracing the toe of his dusty shoe along a crack in the floor as Rodrigo continued.

"It is too late to help in the burial of Pablo and Sixto," Rodrigo said, "but what should we do? We need your voice. There is no other man in the valley who can speak as you speak, no one who will dare to tell the truth as you do."

"Rodrigo...."

"We need your help, Pastor. We need you to speak for us."

He looked up at Rodrigo and then around at the others. They were all looking at him now, and Quetoda felt a sudden stirring in his chest, a wave of hope rising as he felt the once discouraged men begin to coalesce around him. "Do you all agree?" he said. "Do you all feel this way?"

"Yes, Pastor. Yes. We need your help."

"Then I'll give you my thoughts." He thrust his hands into his pockets and leaned back against the dais in front of the pulpit. "First, I think that all your actions should be peaceful," he said. "Then, I think that the Farmers' Syndicate should hold a memorial service for Pablo and Sixto—not only in Baná but all across the country. Let the government know that you want the killers arrested. Let them know of your strength. And let them know that you want the land reform laws observed and enforced."

"Will you help us plan it, Pastor? Will you join us in our public statements?"

For a moment, he could say nothing. And then quite suddenly, as Rodrigo spoke again, "Will you help us?" he could feel their desire picking him up like a wave and carrying him along just as his own anger and zeal had carried him through the sermon on Sunday morning, an emotional wave making it impossible to resist them. "Yes. Yes. I will help you!"

But the men from the Farmers' Syndicate were not the only ones who called on Quetoda that week. The second visitation came on Wednesday night after the midweek prayer service, two men, entering the darkened church and finding him in his study just at the moment before he reached to turn out the light. "Pastor," one of them said at his back. And he jumped in surprise as they emerged from the darkened hallway, one with white hair and wearing a beret, the other thin and leaning heavily on a walking cane.

"Yes?"

"I am Antonio Molina," the white-haired man said. "I am a priest at the cathedral in Baná."

"Father Molina?"

"Yes. My name is Antonio."

"But this is very surprising," Quetoda said. He looked for some sign of Molina's office, but there was not even a cross visible outside his rough peasant shirt. "I never expected a Catholic priest...."

"We are a nation of surprises," Molina said. He reached to shake Quetoda's hand. "This is my colleague, Tomás Rubio."

And then Quetoda recognized the name. "Molina, Antonio Molina—are you the poet?"

"Yes, I write poetry."

"But your poetry is known everywhere!" Quetoda said. "I read it in Guatemala when I was in school!"

"Yes. Perhaps."

"Oh, this is unbelievable! For a Catholic priest to visit a Protestant minister and, and that the priest is Antonio Molina! It's unbelievable!"

"You too have a reputation," Molina said.

"I?"

"At least in the Baná valley."

"I don't understand," Quetoda said. "But sit down, please." He pushed forward two chairs and then returned to sit on the edge of his desk. "Why do you say I have a reputation?"

"Every campesino in the valley has heard of your sermon on Sunday," Molina said.

"Oh."

"I came to meet you and welcome you to Baná."

"Excuse me, but never before have I heard of a Catholic priest welcoming a Protestant—even speaking to him, if he could help it."

Molina laughed. "My bishop won't come, never fear. He would prefer to think you didn't exist. But my bishop and I don't agree on all things."

"Unbelievable!" Quetoda said again.

"Are you familiar with the Second Vatican Council?" Molina said, "the conference at Medellín?"

"I've only heard of it."

"Under Pope John, Twenty-third, the council concluded that the most important Christian witness was in service to the poor. Some of us are ready to recognize *all* Christians who serve the poor—regardless of sect."

"This is like a dream."

"Mind you, the Church is not unified on this subject," Molina said, and there was a hint of laughter in his voice. "Some take the view that those who give handouts to the poor are saints, while those who help the poor to help themselves are communists."

"But I'm not a communist."

"No. Perhaps not."

"And I've never been political."

"Then perhaps you've never been truly Christian, either," Molina said. He rose, smiling broadly and placing his hand on the shoulder of his crippled companion. "It's all right to be political," he said. "Indeed, around here, I don't think you can avoid it. Isn't that right, Tomás?"

Tomás nodded and squinted up at Quetoda through steel-rimmed spectacles as he stood and fumbled at the knee of his left trousers leg to adjust the unseen metal brace that clanked as it slipped into place. "I also welcome you to our cause," he said.

"But remember one thing," Father Molina said. He touched Quetoda's shoulder, squeezing hard in a grip of affectionate firmness. "You are more valuable alive than dead. Sometimes, in our zeal, we let enthusiasm drive us. But it's good also to work behind the scenes, quietly. To win a revolution, one must subordinate zeal to discipline."

"But, I'm not fighting a revolution!"

"Just remember the two dead campesinos," Molina said. "Just remember."

20

Fear. Ever since Segura had left her, Karen had felt it hovering just behind her shoulder like a persistent cloud, and not just fear of Segura. The whole business had placed her totally out of order. She should have known better. She *did* know better. She hadn't meant for any of it to happen. She shouldn't have let him enter her house. Segura, for God's sake! Brutal, deadly, and—she had to admit it—*beautiful* Segura! God help her. And whether it was sensible or not, she had to admit also that somewhere in some deep, dark, or maybe sick part of her soul, she wanted to see him again. Jesus! She hadn't realized she was such a pushover. And then, God help her again, suppose people at the embassy would find out. Rick, for heaven's sake! God, how he would laugh! Rick, pulling one eyebrow up in that little half cocked way of his. No! She had to find a way out of this tangle and make sure she was never alone with Segura again.

Somewhere in the back of her mind, she could see her father in his dress naval uniform throwing up his hands and rising in righteous indignation at the gates of heaven—or wherever it was old navy captains went: "What? Involved with a Latino policeman!? Reprehensible!"

On that morning, she had found herself running to get out of the house where it had all taken place. She wanted to forget the night, wanted to forget Segura, wanted never to see or even think of him again. But when she got to work, she had found a message asking her to return his phone call, and the fear had surged forward again like a pursuing hound that wouldn't let her out of sight.

She found, however, that she felt safer when she was with others, so throughout the morning, she looked for ways to stay publicly busy—talking on the telephone, working with her secretary, coordinating plans with other members of the staff and with the theater for the symphony concert. But, with afternoon and sight of the sun dropping behind the palm in the embassy courtyard, she knew she had to do something to avoid sheer panic.

Maybe Ron Hartley would be able to meet her for dinner, she thought. But then, as she reached for the phone, she stopped, reminding herself most of an awkward twelve-year-old and feeling hotly embarrassed at herself. What was happening to her? she thought. What kind of diplomat was *she* going to make? It was no game for twelve-years-olds. But somewhere in her mind, she had come to count on Hartley as her first line of defense. Surely Segura would keep his distance if she were with another American. But then, in all honesty, she had to admit that she hadn't faced the question of what she would do with Hartley after dinner if she did call him. Would she take him home? God! He was obviously a virile man and he liked her. And she liked him, no doubt about it. But would she have kept him there all night—even slept with him, offered him sex in return for protection?! God, what a crummy thing to do! And then, just how serious was Segura when he threatened to kill any man who touched her?

She floundered. For a moment, she thought of inviting her secretary Antonia to dinner. It would be a nice thing to do. But Antonia wouldn't stay all night. And in any case, just how much defense would a Nicaraguan woman offer against Segura?

And then, just as she was about to decide she would have to go it alone, she heard someone whistling pleasantly in the hall, and Rick appeared in the doorway. "Oh!" she said. "Just the man I want to see."

He looked back mockingly over his shoulder. "You sure you're talkin' to the right guy?"

"Come in and close the door," she said.

"Jesus, a private audience!"

"I've got a social problem," she said.

"I'll never believe it."

She told him about Segura's interest—not about her interest, of course, just that, as she put it, totally without intending to, she had inflamed the captain of the Managua police.

"Inflamed him?"

She began to embroider. "He calls me. He comes by the house. You know, he pops up in strange places and tells me how he wants to be with me, that I'm the most beautiful woman he's ever seen, et cetera, et cetera...."

"Congratulations."

"Rick, I'm serious. This is one I can do without!"

"*Another* one, you mean."

"Rick, I started not to tell you—but you're head of security. I'm doing my job."

He looked across her desk, raising the one eyebrow and smiling now suspiciously and somehow insultingly as she knew he would. "How far has it all gone, Karen? I saw his car in front of your house last night."

"You what!?"

"I saw his car."

"You're checking on me?"

"Well, yes. And I saw his car."

"Why in God's name were you checking on me?"

"Karen...."

"That's the most reprehensible thing I ever heard."

"We check on all our people—especially the women living alone."

"I'm an adult woman. I'm entitled to privacy...."

"Don't talk to me about it. Talk to the ambassador. With all the crazy things going on these days, he wants our people protected."

"Yes, but...."

"What are you hiding, Karen?"

"I'm not hiding anything. Rick, I'm asking for advice."

His eyebrow came down then, and he looked at her soberly, as though at last he was paying full attention.

"It's all kind of delicate," she said.

"O.K."

"I don't want any unpleasant incidents. And I suppose my question is, 'How do you turn off a hot-blooded Spaniard without insulting him?'"

"You probably don't. But I guess I could talk to him—tell him you're unstable and dangerous."

"Rick! Will you be serious?"

"Why do you care what we tell him?"

"I'm going to have to work with him from time to time. I don't want to look incompetent."

"I could tell him you're all mine and order him off the premises."

"He also said he would kill any other man who touched me."

"Oh, well then." He chuckled. "In that case.... Jesus, I thought you'd be an expert at this stuff by now."

And then, in spite of her irritation, they worked out a plan that she would follow meticulously. She would eat dinner before dark and take the phone off the hook and leave the lights off for the rest of the night. Rick or someone else in security would come by to check the premises at least once every hour.

It made for a very long night, but although she woke several times to the sound of cars in the street, it seemed to work. She got through the rest of the night without being seriously disturbed, and by daylight, she felt liberated again, felt that maybe the whole business would just go away now and let her get on with her life as before. But when she reached her office, the pink message slip on her desk corrected all her illusions about freedom: "Captain Segura wants to know what traffic and security police will be required for the symphony concert," it said. The call had been received sharply at eight o'clock, and Karen knew that it would be impossible to avoid Segura any longer. Her day was going to be full. She had to meet Amanda Kingston and arrange for the big reception; she had to arrange the lodging for the symphony musicians. But somewhere in between, she was going to have to face up to Raúl Segura.

She paced to the window, took a deep breath, and returned to the telephone. Airy. That was the mood she'd create. Pleasant. Breezy. Businesslike. Let nothing slip into private seriousness. She dialed and asked for the captain, preparing in her mind all the opening phrases, sallies that would keep him off balance when he answered. "Ah, good morning, Captain Segura. This is Karen Kellner. My secretary told me you called."

She got just that far without stumbling, just far enough to hear his second word, "*Kahren*, why are you treating me this way?" And at the full sound of his voice, she knew exactly why he had been able to maneuver her unresisting into his arms. He spoke English with his Spanish accent, and the dark bass sound of his voice caused a twitch between her shoulder blades that crawled all the way up to the back of her scalp as he continued. "All yesterday I called, and last night. I even met Rick Adams in the streets—who seemed to be guarding you. Are you all right?"

"Yes, Captain." She stumbled, groping. "Yes, my secretary told me, and she's standing right here now," she lied. "I think, I think we will have to talk about those things at another time, on another telephone. This is a business phone, after all, and we'd better, just, discuss business—er, traffic and security."

"I must see you, *Kahren*," he said. "I must talk to you. I think of nothing else...."

"Traffic and security," Karen said. "We must talk of traffic and security." She began to get into her subject, and gradually her momentum began to build. "I have asked Rick Adams to coordinate with you about embassy personnel and automobile traffic around the theater. But of course, you know that President Somoza has accepted our invitation—along with his family and staff—both for the concert and the reception at the Kingstons, and possibly you may want to confer with Colonel Negroponte about that."

But he was not to be deterred. "When will I see you, *Kahren*? When...?"

"I will be at the concert, the reception."

"Then I will see you there."

"Yes, probably, no doubt—I'll call you. We will talk when this is over."

"Will you be alone?"

"Raúl, I will be in a crowd of officials and musicians."

"Who will be your escort?"

"I don't believe...."

"Will it be Mr. Hartley?"

She hedged. "Possibly. Either Mr. Hartley or Mr. Adams. Many things must be arranged and I must go. Rick will call you."

When she hung up, she felt ready for a two-week vacation. "God help me!" she said. She was standing, and she leaned back against the wall and closed her eyes. "I hope I learn something valuable out of all this." And then her telephone was ringing again.

21

By the following day, the changes were coming more rapidly. Quetoda went to his study as usual to prepare his Sunday sermon, but no sooner had he sat down than he heard a knock on the door, and Gaspar was pushing hurriedly into the room followed by a slight brown boy who clutched a bundle of cloth in his arms. "Pastor, it's started!" Gaspar said, and he pushed the boy forward as he closed the door.

"What?" Quetoda said. "What's started?"

"The punishment—the retaliation."

"Where? What happened?"

"The men—the men who went with you to the farms of Agri-21—they were coming home just at daylight when a group of armed men attacked them."

"Jesus help us!"

"Two of our men were killed—and maybe one of theirs when José got him with a machete." Gaspar nodded to the boy by his side.

"You? You killed one of them?!"

"Maybe. Yes, Pastor," the boy said. "At least he's hurt where I cut him across the neck. I got his Tommy gun."

"You what?"

"His Tommy gun. I got it. Look!"

The boy began to unwrap the bundle of cloth, and a moment later the freshly oiled submachine gun lay on Quetoda's desk. "God in heaven help us!" Quetoda said. He felt suddenly sick. "Suppose they find you with that?!"

"It would be very bad."

"We've got to get rid of it. Bury it somewhere."

"Or keep it safe," Gaspar said, "until we get it to proper hands."

"What proper hands?"

"I think something very important will happen soon," Gaspar said.

"What are you talking about?"

"I think we are going to need all the weapons we can find."

"No. Gaspar. No." Quetoda touched the big man's shoulder. "We have to prevent it, if we can. I'm not working for an armed fight."

"Sometimes Fate takes over in spite of us, Pastor."

Quetoda looked again at the submachine gun on his desk. "Did they see your face?" he said to José. "Can they identify you?"

"I don't know."

"Suppose someone followed you here?"

"The men are very frightened," Gaspar said. "Frightened and angry."

"All of us are frightened," Quetoda said. He went to the window and looked out. "What are we going to do?"

"That's why we came to you, Pastor. You know more than anyone."

For a moment Quetoda gazed at the sunlight that glistened on the avocado tree at the end of the garden. "Will you see the men again today?"

"Some of them, yes. I'm working in the tobacco barns tonight."

"Then pass the word." Quetoda turned from the window. "Tell them to come to church on Sunday. Afterward we will have a meeting."

"Here?"

"Here or somewhere."

"Suppose the Guardia also comes to church."

"Then we will be worshipers together in the house of God."

"Are you sure God will be home, Pastor? Sometimes it seems He has gone for a long vacation."

"Then it will be our job to call Him back, won't it?"

Gaspar laughed. "What about the machine gun?"

Quetoda knew what they wanted, and he knew they would never ask directly. "Leave it," he said. "Right where it is and get out of here. I'll hide it."

"But you won't damage it?"

"No, I won't damage it."

When they were gone, he stood for a long time beside the window just staring at the closed door.

A machine gun!

It lay in the center of his desk, dark blue and glistening on its bundle of rags. When he had been a teenager and his father had been in favor with the government of Guatemala for helping solve some mathematical problem, he had been invited by members of the junta to go on hunting trips into the mountains and into the jungles. Of course, at that time, he had been planning to make a career of the army, and he had enjoyed the chance to carry a rifle and learn to shoot. But he had never even touched a submachine gun, and now just the sight of it made his heart beat faster. He went to it, hands still trembling. The magazine was fully loaded, and he clicked the safety off and on and then for a moment held his breath and listened for the sound of any foreign movement in the church. A hiding place. The gun felt cool and solid in his hands. He had to talk to Father Molina about it, find out how to proceed— but in the meantime, a hiding place. He moved then and began to rewrap the gun, turning it on its back like a baby being diapered, taking care that the flowered cloth remained loose enough to hide its shape and then smiling suddenly as he thought of the Bible verse about Mary wrapping the baby Jesus in swaddling clothes. Somewhere safe, he thought, smiling again. Somewhere safe for the gun in swaddling clothes. The last place anyone would look— even Gaspar.

He went to the door, opened it slowly, listened again. Then taking the machine gun, he walked briskly through the hall and into the sanctuary. Beneath the pulpit was a long recess which was used only for a Bible and for notes, and the pulpit cloth covered it like a curtain. He removed the pulpit Bible, slipped the submachine gun deep into the recess, then replaced the Bible and dropped the cloth.

On Sunday, he would deliver his sermon about equality across an unseen, loaded machine gun. His hands smelled of gun oil, and the whole idea made him dizzy. But then he sighed and turned away toward the door. He had to find Father Molina at the cathedral, he thought, before the day was out. There was no way now he could proceed alone.

22

The hardest part was leaving Maria. Eating supper on the porch of their small frame house in the breeze that came down from the mountains before dark, Quetoda watched as she moved through the dusk in her loose cotton smock, filling the air with the flavor of papaya and orange as she brought a pitcher of juice to the table.

"Will you be late?" she asked him.

"No, I don't think so. I just need to talk with Father Molina."

"Why? Has something happened?"

"The Syndicate must make a policy—decide what to do about intimidation on the job," he said. Then he looked away and drank deeply from the glass she had given him, almost escaping into the glass as he had escaped into the word, *intimidation*, consciously avoiding the specifics of two men beaten and shot on the roadside. Intimidation. There was no need to alarm her, he thought, especially on a night he was to be away. He could tell her later. He drank again, remembering suddenly the submachine gun beneath his pulpit. Maybe he wouldn't tell her about that at all. "I must go," he said.

But she sensed the tension in him as he stood. "What's the matter?"

"I just hate to leave you," he said.

"I'll be fine."

"You know I never wanted this job."

She hugged him. "Hurry home."

He heard Father Molina's voice from the hall, even before he had entered the apartment in the stone house behind the cathedral. "There is nothing for it but to strike," Molina was saying. Other men, strange looking men, were coming out as Quetoda arrived, but he found Molina alone at his desk beneath the crucifix on the whitewashed wall, and the priest virtually repeated himself when he turned and saw Quetoda. "A strike. A national strike. Paralyze the whole country. If we fail to resist now, we abandon all hope for the future."

"I agree," Quetoda said. "Hello."

"Yes, my son. Hello." Molina stood and embraced him. "We must move while there is still time. But it must be carefully planned."

"And without violence," Quetoda said.

"Yes. Without violence. A union is not an army. We'll call it a 'Day of Mourning,' a memorial for the murdered men."

"That's perfect," Quetoda said.

Molina motioned to the chair beside his desk. "All areas of the economy must be involved," he said. "The farms, the factories, transportation, clerks in the stores, everyone, even the Guardia."

"The Guardia?"

"Here is a list of demands I have so far."

Quetoda had seen most of the list before: arrest and conviction of the murderers, an end to the harassment of workers, implementation of land reform laws, a national minimum wage, better schools, better medical care. But at the bottom of the page, he found a brand new twist, a request to increase the wages of the Guardia. "Why?" Quetoda said. "Why should we fight for the Guardia?"

"Who makes up the Guardia?"

"What?"

"Campesinos make up the Guardia," Molina said. "Campesinos, that's who. Poor peasant boys who couldn't get work. And why do they steal and pillage and obey cruel leaders? Because they're underpaid." He was standing now, pacing from his desk to the door and back again.

"But their officers?"

"Their officers are butchers," Molina said. "That's another thing altogether. But maybe this effort to increase the soldiers' pay will make them all feel a little less like shooting into our demonstration." He smiled, and as he did, there was a crash in the hall, the sound of someone stumbling over furniture in the dark, and the two men turned as Tomás Rubio entered the room, moving quickly, making a little turn that would be as close as he was ever likely to come to a dance step.

"Tomás!" Molina said. "I thought you were in Managua."

"I was," Rubio said. "But now I'm here. Do you have any food?"

"Yes," Molina said. "Yes. I think there's something left from dinner."

"What's this about dead campesinos? I heard whispers in the bus station."

Molina told him about the roadside killing of the two farmers as he laid out a bowl of vegetable stew and a slice of bread on the kitchen table.

"Animals!" Rubio said. "Animals! Rabid dogs. That's what they are. And you want to have nothing more than a strike? A demonstration?"

"For now," Molina said. "For now. We have to try. But—later— we have to see."

"Maybe we can use it," Rubio said. "Maybe this killing will be the biggest mistake they ever made." And suddenly his tone lightened as he took the first bite of stew. "Is there maybe a taste of sacramental wine? Something to celebrate our action?"

"Why not?" Molina said. "Why not?" He went into the next room and returned with the wine and three glasses. "It couldn't go to a better cause."

"This is really why I associate with a priest," Rubio said, "the availability of free wine." He winked at Quetoda as Molina filled their glasses.

"There is one question that bothers me," Quetoda said.

"What?"

"Suppose the Guardia is not pacified by our efforts to win them higher pay. Suppose, on the day of the demonstration, suppose they simply fire point blank into the ranks of marching workers. What do we do then?"

Rubio was suddenly holding the bread in his fist, waving it like a billy club as he spoke around the bite in his mouth. "Let me tell you," he said. "If they do that...."

"The workers should escape, save themselves as best they can," Molina said.

"...It would be the start of revolution in Nicaragua," Rubio said. "The people's army will be prepared."

"I did not volunteer to fight with the 'people's army,'" Quetoda said.

"If they hurt one of the marchers in your demonstration, then I tell you that every unsuspecting military post in the country will be overrun. Every Guardia soldier who shows himself will be a target. We won't stop till we capture the president himself."

"You can do this?"

"Yes," Rubio said. He waved his bread again. "Do you know what the Farmers' Syndicate is?"

"Tomás," Molina said. "You may be going too far."

"No," Rubio said. "If he works with us, he needs to know everything." He turned back to Quetoda. "The Farmers' Syndicate is the same organization that Sandino used in 1927 to launch his attack against the invading U.S. Marines."

"I've heard of Sandino."

"He held the Marines at bay for five years until the U.S. president recalled them," Rubio said. "And then Sandino worked for peace in Nicaragua until old Somoza-Garcia had him assassinated. And now, we've put his organization back together. So, if this government does not put land reform fully into effect and if they don't find a way to stop the random murders, then this government and *this* Somoza will have to face the ghost of Sandino and the people's army across a battlefield."

"But—even if you're right—all that would come later," Quetoda said. "After the fact. What will we do at the demonstration itself? At the time?" He pointed at Rubio. "Are we just sacrificial lambs to start your revolution?"

"No, my friend, no," Molina said. "We will have a plan. We'll prepare it tonight. The workers will know what to do."

"And what real hope do we have that other unions will join us?" Quetoda said. "Will a bus driver strike because of two dead farmers? Or a telephone operator? Or a bank clerk hurrying home to supper? Will anyone respond besides the farmers?"

"We must try," Molina said. "The framework is there and we must try to use it. But there is much to be done, much preparation."

He forgot totally about the submachine gun. They worked far into that night and over the next few days. And gradually the strike took shape as the old mimeograph machines in both the church and the cathedral turned almost continuously. They prepared circulars and mailed notices to newspapers and government offices. They delivered announcements by hand. They made signs and nailed them to public walls. But the major part of the campaign had to be carried out face to face, and every day Quetoda traveled with three other syndicate workers to visit the fincas in the Baná valley to talk with the workers, owners, and managers. And at almost every gateway, they were rebuffed.

"Why do you continue?" Maria asked him when he came in at the end of the fourth day. "Jonathan, why do you do this to yourself?" He was sitting beneath the light in their living room as she spread disinfectant on his cheek where he had been struck by a rock. "Use the mail. Nail the notices to a tree. Anything but this."

"I'm trying to build a network," he said. "Person to person."

"It's dangerous."

"They have to see we're not afraid to face them," he said.

But of course, he *was* afraid. Waking cold each morning, he could smell the fear on his own body. And as he waited for his fellow workers to come in the car that had been brought from another province, he prayed through clenched teeth for the courage to face the angry owners and managers who saw him only as a troublemaker. And through the first four days, it worked.

But on the fifth day, at the entrance to Agri-21, everything changed. At first, it looked easy because only one man was standing watch at the guardhouse when Quetoda arrived with his three coworkers and asked to see Señor Corico. But the guard resisted. "No puedo," he said. "I can't let you."

Quetoda handed the man a circular and pointed to the last paragraph. "It's on workers' business," he said. "We're even asking to increase the wages of the Guardia."

"Ah sí! Maybe I will call someone." The guard hooked the strap of his carbine over his shoulder and reached for the telephone. But five minutes later, when a black sports van arrived in a swirling column of dust from across the field, it was not Señor Corico but the man called Zia and five other guards who approached them.

"We don't want you here," Zia said as he got out of the van. He was a heavy man with a prominent belly, hitching up his pistol belt as he moved ponderously forward. "I told you that before," he said. And without the slightest warning, he struck, driving his fist hard into Quetoda's mouth. Quetoda went down, and instantly Zia was astride his chest, grabbing his collar with one hand and pounding his face with the other. Around him, Quetoda was dimly aware that his friends were also being beaten in the ditch, but his arms had turned instantly to jelly and he could do nothing but writhe on the ground and try to escape the blows that fell against his face. "Now," Zia said. He stood and snatched a carbine from the guard, and as Quetoda tried to scramble away, Zia planted a booted foot on his shoulder and turned him, practically standing on his chest as he rammed the muzzle fully into Quetoda's mouth, breaking a tooth and driving it gagging hard against the back of his throat. "Next time, I will pull the trigger," Zia said. "Do you understand me? Next time, I will kill you. This time, I will let you go away to tell the others. But don't you ever come back. Now get out of here!"

Somehow they managed to get away, zigzagging along the dusty country roads until they reached Quetoda's house where Maria greeted them in almost total shock as they staggered up the steps. "Jonathan! Oh, Jonathan!" seemed all she could say. "Jonathan!" And then, more with pressure and sign language than with words, she made them all lie on the floor as she cleaned and dressed their wounds, bandaging their cuts and taping the reopened scar across Quetoda's cheek.

He was only half conscious by then, and he resigned himself to her completely, allowing her to lead him into their bedroom and later to hold him in her arms like a mother comforting a sick child, stroking his brow and using her own abundant energy to infuse new life into his body as he lay shocked but still conscious in the darkness. "Jonathan, when can we leave this place? When can we leave before they kill you?"

For a long time he said nothing. But then in a voice that even he did not recognize as his own, he said, "Where would we go? Where? To Guatemala under the Junta? To El Salvador in a widening war?"

"Costa Rica, maybe."

"We would need visas."

"Through the church—maybe the church could get us out."

"Oh, Maria...."

For a few minutes, he drifted off, but he awoke soon in the darkness, still couched like a baby in her arms but staring now into the night, hot eyed with the fever of humiliation that surged like an ocean tide through his body. In that night, with only the sound of her breathing beside him, he knew that no matter how much Maria ministered to his body, no matter how many types of medical aid might be applied to soothe his physical pain, there was nothing which could staunch the internal hemorrhage of shame and rage that he felt toward the man Zia who had violated him so completely. The memory of it now surged and combined with self-loathing at his own contemptible weakness. It gagged him. The taste of it nauseated him as though he were filled with poisonous fluids.

"God help me, God help me," he whispered, but he was strangling on the rage that filled his throat. He turned in his mind to the Bible, searching, as he always did in times of distress, for some word, some direction, that would make his existence tolerable: "Turn the other cheek...," "Love your enemies...," "Bless them that persecute you...." But these words of Jesus stuck in his throat just as his shame and rage stuck in his throat. What he wanted now above all other things was to *kill* his enemy—to crush him—to grind the face of Zia into the earth. He closed his eyes and went on thumbing mentally through the sayings of Jesus: "Shake off the dust of the place from your feet." Yes, that's what he wanted to do, too. He wanted to leave Nicaragua forever, to find some place of peace and order in which to live his life. Shake off the dust. But this verse was quickly followed in his mind by, "He who seeks his life shall lose it, but he that loses his life for my sake shall find it." What did it all mean? he wondered. He felt like the total failure. How could any of it ever be understood? And how could he ever function in public life again?

23

News of the impending strike reached Hartley from the front page of *El Tiempo* in a short article just below a picture of the United States Symphony. "The recent death of two farm workers on the grounds of the Agri-21 consortium has prompted workers to threaten a general strike," the article said. And Hartley read on, his scalp tingling as his eyes moved down the page:

"Agri-21 has been plagued in recent months by worker unrest as workers attempted to increase their wages. Some workers claim that the deaths are the result of management intimidation. But according to Daniel Cortez, brother-in-law of President Somoza and director of Agri-21, there is no relation between the complaints and the killings. 'There are numbers of outside Marxist agitators in the area,' Cortez said. 'We don't yet know the details of this case, but we do know that both workers and supervisors must defend themselves against assault.'"

Hartley was on the phone to Cortez before the hour was out, and he was slightly surprised at his own directness: "What's going on at Agri-21?" he said.

And Cortez was as suave as ever: "It is very tragic, Mr. Hartley," Cortez said. "And, frankly, we don't really know the whole story. Investigators are at work to solve the crime."

"Is there danger they could strike—close down your operation?"

"No. Absolutely not." Cortez chuckled slightly. "Oh, there could be some brief agitation. But let's be realistic, Mr. Hartley. Where would our workers go? No one pays higher wages. We've seen to that. And there are always other workers to be found."

"Wait," Hartley said. "Wait." His voice was suddenly louder. "Obviously something is wrong, and I hope you can find a way to correct it."

"Don't you worry, Mr. Hartley."

"I know workers can be a pain in the ass, but if you have a personnel policy that causes bad blood, you're as much to blame as they are."

For a long moment, Cortez did not reply, and when he did, his voice had a colder edge: "I assure you we have things under control, Mr. Hartley."

"Good. I'm delighted to hear it. I just wanted to let you know that my bank has a continuing interest in your entire operation— seeing it run efficiently. We want to be working together in the future."

"That's very good of you," Cortez said. His voice began to warm again. "Very good, indeed. I know it is difficult for an outsider to understand. But I assure you, we have it under control." And then he laughed fully. "Of course, if you'd find a way to speed up delivery of our tractors, we wouldn't even have these small problems."

Hartley was still sitting on the foot of his bed thinking about Cortez's reply when the telephone rang again, and his spirits were suddenly buoyed by the warm and familiar voice of Liliana Summerfield. "Ron, how are you?"

"Liliana! My God! Hello!" He hadn't talked to her since Billy Summerfield's funeral, but she sounded exactly the same.

"Why haven't you called me?" she said.

"I've been very busy since I got to Managua, but obviously you got my letter."

"Yes. And I've got so much to tell you! I want to see you."

"I wasn't sure whether you were here or in San José."

"Right now, I'm here in Managua trying to set up our new airline office," she said. "I'd like to show it to you."

"Yes. Say when."

They met for lunch at Antojito's, across from the Intercontinental Hotel near the center of town, Liliana somehow brightening the shade beneath the chilimate trees with her smile as she entered the courtyard, "Oh, Ron!" reaching to embrace him. "I'm alive again, really alive. Coming back home was the best decision I ever made."

He knew that she had moved back to join her family in Central America after Billy's death and that she had been working with her family to start a new commuter airline, but aside from one letter, they had not communicated. She still wore Billy's rings on her left hand, but where she had once been quiet and retiring, she now was bursting with energy. And as they found seats beneath the trees, he could feel her vitality like an electric charge. "I loved Billy," she said. "He was the most generously wonderful man I ever knew. But all that time living in the States as his wife—it was like prison, like locking myself up in an old suitcase, and I didn't even know it."

"So you like your work."

"It's more than that. I have relatives and friends. And my cousin Fernando has been very good. He's found good backing for the airline. He'd even buy another plane if he had the pilots. You want a job?"

"Liliana...."

"I know." She laughed. "You've changed your life. But still, I want to show you what we're doing at the airport."

She took him after lunch to their new offices, driving him in her rented car through the twisting streets of the city and out to the flat valley where the airport had been laid out. "There," she said. "There are the waiting rooms for the big international carriers—Pan Am, Tan, Eastern—all cold and sterile. But here...," she pointed to the fresh orange and black paint of the PenAir terminal, "here, everything will be personal."

"Why PenAir?" Hartley said.

"Peninsula Airlines," she said. "We're for the people at home." Stacks of lumber littered the passageway as workers sawed and hammered around them. "Our passengers will know we love them.

And we will be able to take them to any city in Central America or the islands without going to Miami first."

On the ramp, Hartley could see a Cessna 411 and beside it a 310-B and a Brit-Norman Islander, and a Douglas DC-3 already painted in the orange and black of PenAir. "God!" Hartley said. "It's like watching an old movie. Is this where all the old planes go when they die?"

"Yes," she laughed. "The DC-3 needs new upholstery. But otherwise, they're all good planes. We have excellent mechanics."

He walked onto the ramp, sniffing the odors of fuel and lacquer and oil, running his hand along the smooth metal skin of the Cessna's side. "I think the 310 is one of the prettiest twins ever made," he said. "The army still used them in Vietnam when I was there." He climbed onto the wing and peered into the cockpit. "We called them L-23's."

"Fernando bought it from a charter company in Barbados. You want to take a trip?"

He turned back, still kneeling on the walkway at the root of the wing, and for an instant, looking at her perfect mouth, he forgot that she was his dead friend's wife. "What are you trying to do?" he said.

"I suppose I'm not very subtle, am I?"

"No."

"I'm trying to seduce you back into the cockpit."

"Oh," he teased. "For a minute there, I thought you might have just wanted to see *me*."

"Ron, what a thing to say!"

He jumped down, laughing, making it all a joke. "All you want is my body."

"That's not true." She laughed and took his arm as they walked back toward the building. "Not true at all. Oh, I'll admit I had an ulterior motive, but I'd have come to see you, even if I didn't need a pilot."

"O.K. Then remember." He looked at her soberly. "You're talking to a banker now. Banking's my job, and I've got to concentrate on that. Let's go sit down somewhere and have a drink."

"But the truth is, I *do* need a pilot," she said. "Today."

"What?!"

"Today. I need a pilot."

"You're a very difficult woman."

"The 411 is loaded with a shipment that's due in Jinotega as soon as we can get it there, and our pilot's sick."

"What's the matter with him?"

"I don't know. We loaded the plane in San José and got here this morning. Now he says he can't fly. I called him just before lunch."

"Liliana, I'm here to drum up business for the bank. I've just completed a deal for over a million dollars. I'm supposed to be meeting other bankers, businessmen, heads of corporations. I promised my brother."

"I'm asking you to do a favor for a friend, in your spare time."

"I've been trying to get an appointment with a textile manufacturer for this afternoon...."

"It'll all be VFR, an hour, maybe two hours each way. Clear skies. No delays. I've already checked the weather."

He glanced once around the field, and sighed deeply as he looked again at the planes waiting on the ramp. "Take me back to the hotel," he said. "Let me check my calls." Then he shrugged and looked at her. "And find me some up-to-date charts. Maps. Find me the maps before we leave here."

There were two messages at the desk, one from the Masaya Fabric Company and one from Karen at the U.S. Embassy, and Hartley read each one slowly at least twice before turning back to Liliana who was waiting behind him in the lobby. "All right," he said finally. "All right." He waved the messages toward her. "Let me answer these. Then, if everything seems O.K., I'll fly you to Jinotega."

"I'll be forever in your debt. Shall I wait for you here?"

"No, no. Come on up. It shouldn't take but a minute."

The call to Masaya Fabrics was simple. His meeting with

the chairman, Señor Estevez, was confirmed for two o'clock the following day. But the call to Karen was more difficult. She seemed somehow flustered when she heard his voice, fluttery and disorganized, and he wished suddenly that he had left Liliana in the lobby. "Are you all right?" he said.

She cleared her throat. "Yes, of course." But her voice had an artificial airiness about it. "I just wanted to tell you more about the symphony concert and the reception afterward. It's to be at the Kingston estate—at the American Fruit Company plantation...."

"That's wonderful," Hartley said. "My father used to work for them, and I'm looking forward to going out there again."

"There's a—no, that won't...." She was suddenly disorganized again, and she rattled along in unfinished phrases, "The concert's at—oh, hell, I'm trying to, to figure the best way to meet you without...."

"Without what?"

She moved in a new direction. "Before the concert, I have to be at the embassy."

"Shall I meet you there?"

"No. It would be better if I got a ride. I'll meet you at the theater. Do you have a tuxedo?"

"No."

"Oh. Well. It's all right. Would be nice if you did, but it's really not important."

"I hope I won't embarrass you. Maybe I can find one."

"Oh, don't bother." And then she almost blurted into the telephone, as though it really might have been the whole purpose of her call, "What are you doing for dinner tonight?"

"Tonight? Well...." He glanced across the room at Liliana beside the window. "I have an appointment out of town."

"Where?"

"Jinotega."

"My God, that's a long way!"

"Is it?" Liliana was looking at him now, turning suddenly, her face showing concern as he named the place. "I haven't looked at a map," Hartley said. "But we're flying. Wait...." He put his hand over the receiver and spoke to Liliana. "How long will this trip take?"

She shrugged. "Four, five hours."

"I'm not sure we'll get back in time," he said to Karen. And then he looked again at Liliana, hoping she might somehow relent and release him from his promise or at least postpone the journey, but she only smiled. "I'm sorry," he said.

"Yes," Karen said. "I'll just have to find another companion. Or maybe I should dine alone. Maybe that would be good. I'll see you at the concert tomorrow."

When he hung up, Liliana was standing in front of her chair. "I'm sorry to interrupt your love life," she said. "But this is very important to me."

He laughed and touched her shoulder. "You can't interrupt my love life," he said. "I haven't got one. Show me your charts."

"Right." She spread the map on the bed.

"My God! Look at these mountains and jungles. It would take a week by land."

"Not quite," Liliana said. "There's a road. But it's a two- or three-day trip."

He moved the chart to the floor and knelt as he laid a plotter across it. "You know I didn't plan to fly anymore, don't you?"

"I appreciate what you're doing, believe me."

"What are we hauling, by the way?"

"Building supplies."

"Building supplies?"

She nodded. "And mechanical equipment. It's for the Farmers' Syndicate."

"Will there be somebody to unload it?"

"Oh yes. No problem."

At the airport, once he had checked the plane and inspected the cinch straps around the wooden boxes in the cargo compartment, there were no delays. The engines fired without hesitation and, moments later, although it had been nearly a year since he had flown this type of aircraft, Hartley was ticking off the runup checks and pulling onto the active runway with full clearance for takeoff as though no time had passed at all. He slipped the throttle forward and felt the familiar solid pressure in the small of his back as the gathering thrust pushed him against the seat and in seconds they were up over the city with the whole panorama of Central America opening up in the sunlight before them. "Yahoo!" was all he could say. And without thinking about it at all, he leaned over and kissed Liliana on the cheek.

"Not going to fly anymore, eh?" She laughed. "Neither are the birds."

The field at Jinotega was not clearly described on the chart, and when Hartley dropped down to find it behind the mountains, he was surprised to see that it was not paved. "I hope they haven't had any heavy rains lately," he said. And he dropped lower, still under full power at fifty feet, flying just beneath the height of the trees that formed a wall on either side of the landing strip as he surveyed the condition of the runway. But everything looked sound, and with the next approach, he came on in, nursing the plane down as slowly and softly as possible on the main gear, gradually getting the feel of the ground and cutting the power back to brake before the end of the runway, where he turned and taxied back to park in front of the little house that served as a terminal office beside the runway. "Let's open this thing up. It'll be 110 degrees in about two minutes." A slight brown woman and two naked children stood watching them from the shade beside the house. "Doesn't look like your unloading crew is very eager to work."

"They'll be along. Don't worry." Liliana stepped down from the wing and spoke to the woman, but in the local dialect, Hartley could understand nothing until Liliana turned back to him and spoke again in English. "She has a telephone," Liliana told him. "I'll call. She says come in and she'll give us coffee."

They sat at a table in a large central room that obviously had been adapted for use as a waiting room, and by the time the woman had boiled water for their coffee, they could hear the loading crew approaching in a rusty pickup that long ago had dropped its muffler. Their leader was called Castillo and, as Liliana greeted him with a warm embrace at the doorway, Hartley could see the tip of a holster peeping out from beneath the bottom edge of Castillo's guayaberra. "They'll unload while we drink our coffee," Liliana said.

"Great." Hartley shook Castillo's hand and blew into the black coffee that the woman had set beside him on the table. "I'll be right with them."

"There's no need for you to do anything."

"What?"

"Why don't you just rest and drink your coffee and let them handle it."

"Liliana, when I've got a strange crew working around my airplane, I want to keep an eye out."

"Ron, I know Rubén Castillo very well. He knows what to do."

"Oh." He waited, but only for a moment. Outside, he could see a man standing by the wing with his hand on the aileron, and he stood. "In light of recent events, I think I want to be sure," he said. "I'll be right back."

The workman had moved away from the wing by the time Hartley got there, but inside the plane, he found a slight, brown man with bad teeth sweating away over a tie-down on the floor of the rear compartment. The man seemed grateful enough when Hartley showed him how to release the lashing around a heavy box of freight, but after that, the man seemed to resent his presence.

"Why are you watching us, Señor?" Castillo asked at one point.

"Because I'm responsible."

"Who says so?"

"*I* say so."

"The other pilot walked away and let us alone."

"I'm different," Hartley said. And then, in an instant, the whole focus and shape of the afternoon was broken by a commotion that rose beside them in the doorway as the workman with bad teeth shouldered a wooden crate and stumbled as he stepped backward out of the plane. The man staggered two steps forward, trying to catch his balance, but it was too late, and he fell crashing full length to the hard clay where the wooden box split along its seams, spilling six copper-tipped .30 caliber cartridges, gleaming like gold into the sunlight.

"Poncio, you're a fool!" Castillo shouted. He pushed Poncio aside and stooped to collect the escaped cartridges, waving his arms to the others as he rose. "The rest of you—get this mess cleaned up!"

When Hartley looked up again, Liliana was standing on the opposite side of the scurrying men. "Your coffee's getting cold," she said.

For a long time, he could not speak to her. The men unloaded the last crates and drove away, and only then, as the sun dropped behind the trees, did Hartley move back into the shelter of the building and the breeze from the small electric fan that whirred away in the corner of the room. "You lied to me," was the first thing he said. And for a time, Liliana just sat silently across the table as he drank down the black and bitter coffee and asked the woman for another. "You lied to me—deceived me."

"I'm sorry."

"Sorry!? It was illegal, wasn't it? The whole operation was illegal, and you used me. You used our friendship."

She looked down at the floor.

"Liliana, I've been in their goddamned jail once, and I don't want to go back!"

"I think we should not talk so loudly," she said.

But he paid no attention. "What do we do now if Captain Segura and his men are waiting for us on the ramp in Managua?"

"I'm sorry," she said again. "It's all I can say. I thought the cause justified it all."

"Cause!? What cause? You've made me an outlaw!"

She looked around the empty room and spoke in a whisper. "We think there will be a war," she said. "A revolution. Maybe not today, maybe not next week. But soon."

"And you've got your old buddies smuggling ammunition for you. God Almighty! You could at least have asked me, told me what I was getting into."

"I was afraid you'd say no."

"Yes. And I would have." He went into the kitchen and found the woman with the coffee. "Mas, por favor—tan pronto como es posible," he said. The coffee was steaming, thick and black and spilling over the side of his mug as he returned. "God! It's bad enough to be taken by strangers—but a friend! Jesus!"

"Have I hurt you, Ronald?"

"Hurt me? Yes, you've hurt me. What the hell kind of question is that?"

"No. I mean *really*," Liliana said, and now there was no tone of apology in her voice. "*Really*. Have I hurt you in any real way?"

"Not physically, no. But—*trust*. I trusted you, and now I can't."

"If that box had not opened...."

"So what are you saying—that it's all right to commit any kind of crime as long as you don't know what you're doing?"

"You're very *righteous*, did you know that?"

"What?"

"*Self-righteous*. Your little trust has been upset."

"Now wait."

"Let me tell you something. In this country, people have been tortured, people have had their lands stolen, people have been murdered. Every day, people are starving. I'm working to change that. But you're angry because I didn't tell you everything I knew."

"Wait."

"I lied. Yes. I didn't have a sick pilot. I gave him two days off because I can't trust him. I went to you, my old friend, and asked you to do me a favor because I knew, even if you found out what we were doing, we'd still be safe."

"You risked my life."

"You risk your life every time you walk through the streets of Managua."

"Oh, Liliana, be reasonable...."

"But I did not lie when I told you we were carrying building materials and machinery, because bullets and guns are the building materials of revolution."

"Oh my God!"

"You just didn't ask what we were building."

Suddenly he felt like laughing, and he could no longer hold on to his anger. The whole business seemed so totally preposterous. "You've got an answer for everything, haven't you? An answer for *everything*." He looked out at the sun now angling through the trees, and the coffee felt suddenly like something congealed on the back of his tongue. "We'd better start back," he said. "But sometime I'd really like to know how in hell you got mixed up with all this?"

"Wait," she said. She touched his arm and looked out at the sky. "Now you've got me worried. I don't want to get you in trouble. Maybe we should fly to San José."

"San José!"

"Yes. That way, no one will know about this trip. You can stay at my house tonight and then fly back to Managua in the morning— the usual kind of shuttle trip."

"Jesus!" Hartley said. "What next? Pull out the maps."

They arrived just after dark, taking the whole trip in smooth air until they slipped into the natural wind tunnel that somehow concentrated its energies along the San José runway where a gust suddenly dropped the plane in hard on one gear to add an unexpected bounce to the landing. But there was no damage, and they got through customs quickly. And then, after the silent taxi ride and the nearly silent supper of arroz con pollo that Liliana prepared in her tiny house on the outskirts of the town, she leaned across the table and touched his hand. "I suppose I owe you an explanation," she said.

"Yes," he said. "I think you do."

"It's hard," she said. "And dangerous."

"Dangerous to tell me?"

She took her water glass and walked to the window to look out at the lights across the valley. "Did you ever wonder why I live in

San José and not in Managua?"

"Yes. As a matter of fact, I did."

"Because, there, it would be impossible." She turned then and leaned back against the window sill. "I have to talk slowly because this is difficult for me," she said. "But in the last Nicaraguan election, six years ago, my father, who was a professor at the university, spoke out strongly against President Somoza. He was quoted in the papers. He developed a following and stirred a lot of controversy. And then one night, my brother came home to find both my father and my mother shot to death."

"My God!"

"The crime has never been solved. I was away, working for Aeronica Airways at the time. And that's when I met Billy and married him."

"I knew there had been some tragedy with your parents," Hartley said, "but you never talked about it."

"Some people talk—some don't." She took a swallow of water. "It's hard to realize how young and innocent I was then. I knew nothing about politics. I had been raised in the middle class—the upper class. My father was a very enlightened man who encouraged his daughter to have a career. Our life was good—unless we got out of line. And that was the part I didn't understand until my brother found, without doubt, that our parents had been murdered by the followers of Somoza. I think my father had had enough. He had accepted his pay and his comfortable life almost as a bribe to keep silent until his children were grown. And then he spoke out against the corruption. It cost him and my mother their lives."

"It must have been very hard for you."

"I felt like a refugee. After their funeral, I married Billy, and became a U.S. citizen, a housewife. Changed my life. But my brother stayed. He's a teacher, like our father, but his main job, his life's work, is to build a revolution."

"Where is your brother now?"

"You met him this afternoon—Rubén Castillo."

"You're just full of surprises, aren't you?"

"When Billy died—and my cousin Fernando came to offer me a

job—I had to make some decisions," Liliana said.

"Is Fernando in this, too?"

"No. Oh, say he prefers not to know what my brother and I may do, so long as the airline functions. You realize I'm telling you enough to destroy us all, don't you?"

"Liliana...." He stood and went to join her at the window.

"One word, *one word* could kill us."

"Just don't ever lie to me again," Hartley said. "Don't ever lie."

"Why should I? You're one of us now."

"I am not!" He looked at her and spoke as firmly as he could without raising his voice. "I'm not. That trip does not make me one of you. I am not a revolutionary. I'm a banker. I've fought all the wars I need to fight. Understand that. I'm here to lend money so farmers can buy machinery. I'm here to save my brother's bad bank loan."

"I hear you," Liliana said. "I understand. I'm sorry, but I understand. I'll never violate your trust again." She stood on tiptoe and kissed his cheek. "And now, I think we need some rest."

She put him in her guest room, but he had been there only long enough to take off his shoes before he heard her knock again at the door. She was already in her nightgown and with a kind of flowered shawl around her shoulders, but in spite of her wide mouth and full bosom, she reminded him somehow of a lost child. "I brought you another towel," she said. She laid the towel across a chair and turned to face him. "You do forgive me, don't you?" she said.

"Forgive you? There's nothing...."

"Oh, Ron...." And suddenly she was pressed against his chest. "I feel very cold. Would you hold me for a minute?"

"Yes. Of course. Why don't we get under the blanket?" She did not resist as he guided her toward the bed and slipped in beside her, but as he took her in his arms, he realized that her skin was deeply chilled. "You weren't kidding, were you?"

"No."

He held her close with the desire to comfort her, but he had not lain beside a woman for a very long time, and in spite of her cold, his whole body began to recall lost sensations. He felt her breasts against his chest and the deep cinch of her small waist above her hips, and he inhaled sharply, almost as a sigh in the darkness as she began to warm in his arms. "God, you feel wonderful!" he said. His heart was pounding and suddenly his desire for her was in full flood as he turned her head to kiss her. But her cheek was wet with tears.

"Do you forgive me?" she said. "Do you?"

"Liliana, yes, yes, of course." He kissed the salt of her cheeks, and then suddenly, blindingly, for the first time in many days, he was back at Agecroft Airfield gazing in horror at the fireball on the end of Runway 33 as Billy Summerfield burned to death in the inverted Beechcraft. "Oh Jesus!" And his lust for Billy's widow dissipated like ground fog in sunlight.

In that moment, though he did not move or speak, he was simply overcome with lamentation—for her, for Billy, for the airline they had run together, for his own lost marriage, for Liliana's parents, for all the men whose bodies he had carried out of combat, for the whole sad chronicle of his failures, and he was suddenly fighting to hold back his own tears.

She never asked what happened. She warmed and drifted off to sleep in his arms. But when he woke after sunrise and heard her calling him to breakfast from the door of the room, he knew that he was achingly, overwhelmingly, poundingly in love with Liliana Castillo Summerfield.

24

When Quetoda left his bed two days after the beating, he could hardly stand alone. Maria held him upright until he made it all the way to the front porch where he could stand supporting himself with his hand against a post. But after a brief time, he turned back toward his bed, moving painfully through the house, touching each piece of furniture for balance as he passed. "You have to keep on," Maria told him. "You need the exercise."

But in the bedroom, he fell again across the sheet that now was warm from the midday heat. "I don't want to see anyone," he said, "don't want anyone to see me." But he knew, even as he spoke, that he should have to see Molina. And some way he would have to see Gaspar and the others also, maybe even before the day was out. They had to know what he was going to do. He felt ashamed at the thought. He had failed them, would fail them even more. Now he knew very clearly that he wanted out. Things might one day improve in the Baná valley—or in all Nicaragua. But first they would get worse. He had to accept that now. He could see no way around greater violence. But he wanted out before it happened. He wanted Maria out. He would write to the church and ask for help. He would go to a safer place. And in the meantime—since he had become such an obvious target—he would keep out of sight, become as invisible as possible so long as he remained in Nicaragua.

Still, he had to tell the others, and against the racking objection of his body, he pulled himself from the bed and began to walk again. "Come on," Maria said. "I'll help you."

She gave him vegetable soup and baked chicken that a woman in the parish had brought when she heard he was sick and, by late afternoon, he was moving almost normally, walking through the house, and even to the church and back, until finally in the evening he told her: "I have to see Father Molina."

"Yes. Maybe tomorrow you'll feel well enough."

"Tomorrow will be too late," he said. "I have to see him now, tonight."

Suddenly she was angry, slamming her plate against the table as she stood beside him. "No! Jonathan, you can't."

"Yes, I...."

"It can wait."

"No, I have to...."

"Nothing is important enough to take you out tonight!"

"They are counting on me. I have to let them know I'm out."

"Surely they know that already."

"No. I have to see them."

"Jonathan, it's insane!"

He stood and began to walk again, leaving her nearly shouting at his back as he moved toward the church. "When will you learn? Will you wait till they kill you?!"

But he continued on to his study, and a few moments later found himself in the sanctuary, walking aimlessly into the quiet space and stopping to listen. Would he preach a sermon there on Sunday? Maybe Maria or one of the elders would just lead the congregation in prayer. He stood behind the pulpit, and then, totally without premeditation, he removed the pulpit Bible from its shelf and slipped his hand deep into the recess. The submachine gun was still there, cool and hard, and when he pulled back his hand, it smelled again of gun oil. He sighed and replaced the Bible and turned away. Gaspar would have to take the gun away—somewhere as far as possible, soon.

After dark, against all Maria's objections, he was determined to try it.

"I'll go with you," she insisted.

But on this he was even more adamant. "No. Absolutely not. Suppose I should have car trouble. Suppose I met.... It's no place for a woman, out at night. Lock the doors. Stay here out of danger."

And he left her, taking the old Chevrolet that the union workers had brought to the church and driving down the dusty road with the whole car vibrating from a misfiring cylinder as he moved toward the town.

The cathedral was dark, but he found Molina alone in his quarters reading under a small lamp. "Yes?" Molina said as he entered, and Quetoda could sense that the priest did not recognize him. Molina squinted through the darkness with his white hair forming a kind of halo against the lamp at his back. "Yes?" he said again. And then he gasped as Quetoda came closer. "My God! Jonathan, look at you! Here. Sit down." He pushed a chair forward. "I heard there was trouble but...."

"I have failed," Quetoda said. And suddenly he was weeping, silently, making no move to sit, just standing there with tears streaming down his bruised and swollen cheeks.

"Jonathan!"

"I have failed," he said again.

Molina touched his shoulder, and suddenly Quetoda was sobbing like a child against the older man's chest.

"Jonathan...."

"I've failed. I can't do it. No one can. Nobody can fight armed men with nothing but bare hands."

"Sit down," Molina said again. "You've done all you could. You've been very courageous."

"But no more, Father. No more. I'm finished. I can't do it anymore. I don't think anyone should."

Molina nodded and was silent for a long moment. "It is very hard, I know," he said finally. "But the strike is still scheduled as before."

"I won't be there."

"The men are counting on you."

"I don't care."

"They look up to you. They need your guidance."

"They'll have to look elsewhere."

"There is some rum," Molina said. "I'll get it." He walked into the next room and returned with glasses and a bottle of Flor de Caña. "Sometimes we have to raise our spirits artificially," he said. "Now." He lifted his glass. "To quick recovery."

"Thank you." The rum was hot and sweet, but very good against the back of his throat. "I've been in hell," Quetoda said.

"Yes. I'm sorry. But you're not alone. Even our Savior knows what it's like in hell."

"Our Savior!" Quetoda said. "Where was Our Savior when Zia had his rifle down my throat?"

Molina shook his head and sipped as he sat back in his chair. "If I could answer that question—well, we would know a great deal, wouldn't we? 'Where was Jesus when I needed Him?' How many times I've been asked that question! But you know, the older I get, the more I think that Jesus doesn't do anything to save us at all anymore. Oh, He's there. Don't misunderstand me. I believe He's there. In the next world, waiting for us. And I fully expect to be with Jesus when I die. But I don't believe He does anything for us in this world now. He's already done it. In Judea and Jerusalem, long ago. He taught us everything we need to know about how to live and save ourselves. And now I think it's up to us. We either do it or we fail to do it."

Quetoda sat back then, sipping the warm rum in the dim light, almost hypnotized by Molina's musical voice. Molina was saying almost the same thing he himself had said, in the big sermon that had changed his life. "You are God's hands," he had told his congregation. "Don't expect God to do it for you. You are God's hands." And now he was acting as though he didn't believe it.

"Sometimes it's very difficult," Molina continued. He picked up the bottle and poured another round of Flor de Caña. "Loving God and your neighbor is very difficult. Making the world better, saving it, is very difficult. It requires turning the other cheek, leaving father and mother, leaving wife and home in order to do it. Even laying down your life for a friend. This is the part most evangelists don't talk much about. It's hard."

"You make me feel very ashamed," Quetoda said.

"Ashamed? You? No. You have no reason to feel ashamed. You've certainly proved yourself. You've gone the extra mile, if anyone has."

"You're taking me to task for my cowardice and I know it."

Molina smiled. "The man who isn't afraid is a fool."

"You're more gentle than I deserve."

"I've simply mentioned some things I know we both believe."

Quetoda felt somehow stronger then. Maybe it was Molina, he thought. Calmness seemed to surround the man wherever he went. Or maybe it was the rum. But he stood now, forcing his bruised body to do his will as he moved around the room. "The strike," he said. "Everything is still as before?"

"Yes," Molina said. "Almost. Except that the people in the cities are not so eager. The office workers say *no*, absolutely. They prefer not to be involved. So do telephone workers."

"Then the strike can't be a success!"

"Say rather, it won't be complete. But it has to be carried out, Jonathan. It has to be carried out. The Farmers' Syndicate supports it to a man. And we can't call ourselves Christians and sit quietly by while our people are systematically murdered." Quetoda looked away, but Molina stood and came to him in the shadows, touching his shoulder and turning him to look into his eyes. "Will you be there, Jonathan? Will you be beside me in the demonstration?"

Quetoda wanted to run then, actually wanted to bolt and run from the room, but he could not pull himself away from the penetrating gaze of the older man. "Yes," he said finally. He glanced at the floor then back into Molina's eyes. "Yes. You give me no choice."

He left then, driving slowly through the dimly lighted streets in the old Chevrolet that seemed to vibrate more than ever from the misfiring engine as he turned onto the dusty road toward home. He had felt momentarily better in the presence of Molina, but now, as he drove alone through the night, the prospect of the strike filled him with terror. If the strike worked, it would be a time of rejoicing, a possible rebirth of justice in Nicaragua. But if not.... He had heard stories: "The Guardia gives no quarter." And he would be in the first rank against their rifles.

He left the town, passing nothing but fields and forests and an occasional darkened house beside the road until in the distance he could see the white church and the welcoming light of his own house like a beacon in the night. He rounded the church with relief, pulling fully into first gear as the car bucked against the sand, and then, coming into clear sight of the house, his heart stopped cold as his headlights flashed full on the rear of a black sports van parked beside the porch. The door of the van was open and he could see two men running from the house to the waiting car. "Oh my God! Maria!"

Everything happened very fast, the van spinning its wheels and accelerating in a cloud of dust as Quetoda leapt from his car and ran, calling Maria as he bounded up the steps and then screaming at the top of his voice as he came through the shattered door and into the house, "Maria!"

From that moment, he would not speak clearly again for days. Maria was lying on the living room floor, her neck twisted oddly against the leg of a chair, her dress torn open, and her underpants and one shoe lying in a pool of blood that still flowed fresh around the knife that had ripped her belly from crotch to breastbone. "Maria!" He fell to his knees in the blood at her feet and then, unable to breathe another breath, he blacked out completely and fell across her body.

When he came to minutes later, he moved in a trance. He was covered with Maria's blood, and from somewhere deep inside him came a sound like an animal whimpering as he touched her face, "MariaMariaMariaGodGodGodNoNoNo...," a kind of ritual moan repeated again and again, and he knew from the roots of his being that he no longer cared to live on this earth. *He* was the target. *He* was the one they should have killed. But she had died instead, and *he* had not even been present to deflect her agony. He staggered up, lurching across the room, leaving bloody footprints as he moved through the house toward the church. He *knew* the van that had brought the killers. He had seen it beside the blockhouse at Agri-21 on the day he had escorted the men to ask for higher wages. He had seen it on the day they beat him, the black van with the words "Cherokee Chief" stamped on the rear. He knew!

He moved on through the church, and at the pulpit there was no hesitation. He flung away the pulpit cloth and swept aside the Bible, leaving a bloody thumbprint on its fly leaf as he grabbed for the submachine gun. Then once again he passed through the house, stopping just long enough to kiss Maria's cold and contorted face before he moved on to the old car, still standing in the road with its door open as he had left it.

He drove with the submachine gun across his lap, urging the trembling car through the dark and abandoned streets of Baná and on beside the railroad track of the American Fruit Company and out again into the countryside until in the distance he saw the lights of the guardhouse at the entrance to Agri-21. He drove slowly, pulling into lower gear to keep the old car from lugging with the strain, making a series of zigzag turns to cast his light in all possible directions as he came to the house itself, searching, swinging left and then right, seeing nothing at first, no sign of life and nothing familiar until at last he caught a glint of silver from the back side of the house and saw unmistakably the hood of a Cherokee Chief in the shadows beside the road.

He took his foot off the accelerator altogether, turned off his lights, and drifted to a stop a quarter mile away. For a minute, he just sat there waiting, staring into the darkness as the frogs gulped loudly in the ditch beside him. Then checking one last time to make sure the safety of the gun was in firing position, he made his way slowly back through the darkness toward the guardhouse. The windows were open, and he could hear the fans humming and the sounds of a radio and loud talking and laughter from the main room where six men were gathered, some in T-shirts and some shirtless, men standing in their undershorts beside a card table, all seeming to talk at once as Quetoda walked around the house and gave one single knock at the door.

Someone yelled an answer, and a man in a stained T-shirt turned to open the screen. From that moment, everything unfolded in a kind of slow motion as Quetoda leveled the machine gun and stitched three red holes across the tee shirt in the doorway. The man went down, leaving the others in clear, panic-stricken view, and it was Zia himself who stood at the center of the room in open-mouthed horror as Quetoda took another step forward and the room exploded with the noise as he pressed the trigger, spraying the paralyzed men like flies, dropping Zia across the table, dropping another in the doorway at the back, another in a corner, and the others piled contorted on the floor beside the window.

His ears were ringing as he kicked the first man's body away from his foot. Then slowly and deliberately, Quetoda gathered the three submachine guns and four carbines from the rack on the wall of the blockhouse and slipped out into the night.

25

Hartley did not realize that he was daydreaming until they were in sight of Managua Airport and Liliana was shaking his right arm. "Ron, they're calling us," she said. "They called us twice."

She pointed to the radios, and he realized that he had completely ignored the Spanish voices from the tower: "Nine-one-nine, do you have the field in sight?"

"Oh." He answered the tower, then shook his head as they cleared him to land. "Good thing you're along to keep me awake," he said to Liliana. "'Course, if you weren't along, I might not have been daydreaming in the first place." He laughed and brought the plane in, but as he pulled up to the PenAir ramp and unbuckled his seat belt, his laughter vanished altogether. "This is absolutely crazy," he said.

"Don't say another word," she said, "not a word."

"Liliana...."

She smiled and touched her fingers gently to his lips. "I have to be back in San José tonight."

"When will I see you again?"

He caught her fingers and held them, but she was already looking outside the cockpit and nodding across his shoulder. "I hope you'll see me as soon as we get past those soldiers who seem to be guarding the building."

He turned then and saw them, a large number of them, coming and going all along the taxi way, soldiers with M-16's at every entrance. "What do you suggest?"

"I think we act normal," she said.

And she was right. The Guardia sergeant beside the door asked for their credentials, but at the sight of the U.S. passports, he merely smiled and wished them a good day as they passed on through the construction area and out again into the sunlight. "Something's happened," Liliana said. "I don't know what. But let's move."

He stopped her finally in the parking lot, in the direct glare of the midday sun as she opened the car door. "When?" he said.

"Ron...."

He knew from her tone that she wanted to put him off, but she did not resist as he pushed her against the side of the car and kissed her. "When?" he said again. "Last night you slept in my arms...."

"Ron...."

"There is more."

"I shouldn't have done it. Things are so complicated, so dangerous."

"You can't just breeze into town, trick me into gun running, make me fall in love with you, and then just breeze right out again," he said.

"I'll be back."

"When?"

"I don't know."

"Did you feel *nothing* last night?"

"Of course I felt something last night! Ron...." She kissed him now, very tenderly, her lips soft and moist against his. "Ron, you've been my closest friend. It was you, more than anybody, after Billy died. Last night I felt almost like I was married to you, but Ron, I'm afraid—I'm afraid to go one step further."

"We can't just pretend nothing happened."

"By the time I come back, you'll probably be in the States," she said.

"Then you could come with me."

"What about the work I'm doing here?"

"Jesus! Liliana, I'll be working here too...."

"In the middle of a revolution?"

"Damn it! I don't believe...."

"Think about it, Ron. If a war comes...."

"Two people don't fall in love and then just shake hands and go separate ways like a couple of business acquaintances."

"Will you stay with me? Will you fly for me?"

"What?"

"If war comes to Nicaragua and you're here—will you fly for the revolution?"

"Jesus! What are you asking?"

"Just that. If we lived together—if we married—would you work for the revolution—would you stay with me, possibly in combat?"

"Liliana, I've fought all the wars I need to fight."

"Then, that's our answer," she said. She reached up and took his face in her hands. "Don't you see, my darling? That's our answer."

"I don't see anything except...."

"And I don't blame you a bit. But if you're working for the banks—don't you see? If you're working with the Somoza crowd, Somoza and Negroponte and Cortez and the big business people, you'll be working for our enemies...."

"No!"

"You wouldn't mean to do it. But you'd be doing it, just the same. That's the way the world gets twisted. Just doing your job with the best intentions, you'd still be supporting people who would kill me."

"I'd just be trying to make a living."

"And so would we—except that it's all so unbalanced. The people you work with want to get rich by making my people live like animals."

"I just don't believe it," he said. "They may not be *nice* people, but I can't believe they're as bad as you say."

"But you can believe that this sun is hot, can't you?" She laughed, and he was able to relax.

"I thought it was just me being close to you," he said.

"Get in and I'll take you to town."

When he got out of the car at the hotel, he felt that he was leaving half of himself beside her on the seat. "I can't believe I'm doing this," he said. "I can't believe you're just driving away...."

"Maybe something will happen," Liliana said. She kissed him and touched his cheek through the driver's window. "Maybe after the strike tomorrow, the government will change their ways." She almost laughed. "Maybe I'll get disillusioned and quit. Maybe you'll give up your job with the bank. Maybe we'll just run away to Barbados and live on the beach and pretend there are no problems in the world. But I will be back," she said. "There's no *maybe* about that. I will. I promise." And then she was gone.

Even before he checked for messages, he found a table on the veranda and dropped into the chair with his flight bag still across his shoulder. "Rum," he told the waiter. "Rum with orange. Double. Ron con jugo de naranja." Jesus! he thought. It had all hit him in a way he least expected. Not only was it her beauty but something else that made his ears tingle. Somehow her small frame had become bigger than life, almost transfigured, taking on a strange light as she spoke of her *work*. It was spellbinding. God! What could happen? He had met true believers in the jungles of Vietnam. They could be burned, shelled, and shot, and still they were undeterred. It was both inspiring and frightening, but in this woman...!

"These are the choices," she had told him. "In this part of the world, there's no middle ground. You either work for change so life can be better for all people or you work to maintain the status quo and keep wealth among the few. Those are the choices. And one side will destroy the other." She had always seemed so soft and vulnerable, he thought, but now there was something in her like spring steel. Coming back to Latin America, she had developed a hardness, a suit of invisible armor. And yet, she had felt so totally vulnerable against him in the night.

The rum was soothing against his throat. But now he felt a deep sadness as he sat there looking out at the thorns of the Cruz de Cristo tree. Everything seemed totally impossible. He had been to war; he had played the soldier of fortune, and now he was thirty-seven years old with nothing to show for it except the knowledge that the world was an enormous Catherine wheel that would wrack its people to the limits of possibility, if it could. He wanted to break that cycle—not run back into another war. "Would you fly for the revolution?" Liliana had asked. And the thought made him shiver. No! Never again. Too often he had waked in a sweat, dreaming of tracers at night along the Cambodian border. Jesus! Planning a war could only be done by the ignorant, the insane, and the desperate. Or, oh yes, he thought, it could also be planned by the saintly. He mustn't forget that. It could be planned and run by the saintly, by the true believers whose faith in their cause was so great that all other life became irrelevant.

But now he heard English in the air, and he realized that the people coming and going around him were carrying musical instruments as they came from the theater across the square, and he remembered Karen and the symphony concert. Time to get back to real life, he thought. The last twenty-four hours had been a total deviation. Gun running, for God's sake! This afternoon, he had to keep his appointment with Masaya Fabrics.

He walked into the lobby, now moving with dispatch, all business as he took the message slip which the clerk handed him: "Tractors shipped from Norfolk yesterday—Brad." And then, as he nodded with satisfaction and turned toward his room, he glanced at the large black headlines of the newspaper that lay on the far end of the counter: "Blood Bath at Agri-21."

26

Quetoda would never remember how he got there, but suddenly, as though waking from sleep, he found himself in front of Gaspar's door, shouting and beating against the roughhewn wood of the cave house, "Gaspar! Gaspar!" shouting through the darkness like a man drunk or insane, until, with sudden violence and totally without warning, he felt the barrel of a pistol against his spine and an arm around his throat cutting off his breath as a voice from behind whispered through clenched teeth, "If you so much as move, I will kill you."

"Gaspar," he choked.

And then the big man recognized him, seeming even in the darkness to sense his catastrophe as he released his hold, "Pastor! You've been hurt!"

"No, no. Not me. They didn't hurt me...."

"Come in." Gaspar opened the door, and in the flare of the lantern light, he could see for the first time the pile of weapons at Quetoda's feet. "My God! How did you get them?"

"Help me," Quetoda said, handing one submachine gun and then another toward Gaspar. "Take them—take them wherever they need to go and *use* them. Use them!" He was shouting as he came into the light, "Use them!" seeming unable to restrain himself even at the sight of Gaspar's wife and two small children peering at him from the rear of the room. And then Quetoda was on his knees, weeping and leaning over the pile of machine guns and rifles on the floor— "Take them...," holding one of the carbines above his head— "Take them..., kill them!"

But Gaspar was trying to lift him to his feet. "Pastor, you've been hurt. Let me help you."

"No, no." He looked down now, seeing truly for the first time the front of his shirt stiffened with blood, studying it for a moment as something totally strange, then suddenly clawing it, wrenching and tearing the shirt from his chest and holding the bloodstained tatters lovingly against his face as his voice rose in a wail through the dim light, "Mariaaa! Maria! They killed Maria! It's Maria's blood, not mine. They killed her!"

And then Gaspar was on his knees beside him, holding Quetoda in powerful arms as though subduing a child or an animal gone berserk, but speaking softly, "Pastor, let me help you. Let's clean you up."

Quetoda surrendered then as Gaspar signaled for his wife to come forward, and together they led him into the yard and bathed him by lantern light, washing the blood from his face and body as Quetoda told of taking the submachine gun from the church and tracing the Cherokee Chief to Agri-21, telling them, almost chanting as he spoke of walking into the block house and of the six men collapsing and sprawling before him. "I could not have lived if I hadn't punished them," he said. "I would have killed myself— myself or them." And then as Gaspar handed him a suit of his own oversized work clothes to wear, Quetoda spun suddenly, grasping Gaspar by the arm. "Gaspar, I have to go back."

"What?"

"Maria—I have to go back for Maria!"

"Pastor...."

"I have to bury her."

"They will kill you if you go back."

"But she has to be cared for."

"I will take care of it," Gaspar said. "I will, or Hilda will." He nodded toward his wife.

"But I can't ask anyone else to take that risk," Quetoda said.

"Pastor, you've put your own life in danger to help the people of

Baná. Now let us help you."

"But...."

"This time, let us help you." He pulled the loose-fitting guayaberra around Quetoda's shoulders. "Tonight, Tomás Rubio is leaving with a troop of men for Jinotega. You must leave with them."

"Not until I know Maria is safely...."

"Pastor, to save your life!" He took Quetoda firmly by the shoulders and looked into his eyes. "To save your life. Tomorrow I or the women will see to Maria."

27

It was the subject that would dominate the rest of the day, "The Blood Bath at Agri-21." Both Cortez and Colonel Negroponte were unavailable when Hartley tried to call them, but signs of public shock at the killings were everywhere. Newspapers, television, radio, clerks in the shops. Even Mr. Estevez at Masaya Fabrics—who turned out to be as North American as Hartley—was unnerved. "I mean, Jesus! What do ya' make of it all?" was the second thing Estevez said after hello. He pointed to the headlines of *La Prensa* on his desk, "Rebel Forces Strike Peaceful Farm." "I'd really hate to see this country go like El Salvador. I mean, the rebels there made it just about impossible to do business."

"The people at Agri-21 say everything's under control," Hartley said.

"Jesus! I hope so," Estevez said. "I mean, if the political lid stays on, we've got one of the sweetest deals in the world here—which is what I want to talk to you about."

And when Hartley left an hour later, he could not help agreeing that Estevez did indeed have a sweet deal, so sweet, in fact, that for a while it took Hartley's mind completely off Agri-21. Masaya Fabrics made "Blue Thunder" jeans, one of the hottest new items on the U.S. clothing market. "Our operation's simple and profitable, but it's time to expand," Estevez said. "We bring the cloth down here, already cut to size from the plant in New Jersey. All we do here is sew it up. I mean, you can see what a difference it makes. In Jersey, we'd have to pay workers eight to twenty dollars an hour—

more. But down here—Jesus! —we can hire these peasant women for three dollars a *day*. I mean it. Three dollars! Less. Gives us a big edge over every other jean on the market. I mean, it's the thing that gives me hope, you know. Regardless of politics. If I had to cut back to even half the work I do now, I could still make a profit. But why stop, I say. Why stop? I want to double it. Rebels or no rebels. I want to borrow the money and expand now while everything's hot. I think the sky's the limit. And this can be a damn fine country to live in, too, if they'll just lay off and let us be."

"Let me study this and talk to the people back home," Hartley said. And he took the proposal and the figures under his arm when he left Estevez's office. But already, as he walked out and moved through the fashionable district near the Mayan Hotel, where he had first met the officers of Agri-21, he knew that this would be the kind of deal to gladden Brad's heart. Clearly, it could earn the bank a very healthy profit. *If* the figures tallied and *if*, as Estevez said, the political lid stayed on.

Yet somewhere inside himself, Hartley knew he didn't like it. The Masaya operation was a clear example of what Liliana had been talking about earlier—of one side getting rich while the other was held at the edge of starvation. Masaya Fabrics might expand and the owners grow rich as Croesus, but the workers' wages would stay at three dollars a day forever. It was reprehensible. No doubt about it. Prices were just as high in Nicaragua as they were in the States, and nobody could live on three dollars a day. It was the stuff revolutions were made of. But what was *he* supposed to do about it, he wondered, just quit doing business till the world got better? Well, it would take a lot of waiting. What did those rebels hope to accomplish by killing six guards at Agri-21? Violence just destroyed everything, he thought. And he felt a sudden flare of anger at Liliana for suggesting that he help her in this "revolution" she was dreaming about. He understood her anger and frustration, but it was impossible. He couldn't save the world! He'd tried it once in the Far East, and it had all collapsed in a bloody mess. What he wanted now was to make a decent living, maybe even marry again, and finally settle down in the good graces of his family. God! Brad was right. He had to look out for his sentimental streak, his tendency always to sympathize with the underdog. And he almost wished now that Liliana had never come back into his life. He'd been looking forward to this evening with Karen before Liliana appeared—really looking forward to the concert and the trip to the Kingston's house, and then Liliana had walked in and totally twisted his thinking. He felt love for her, no doubt about it, and sympathy for the peasant workers she wanted to help. But God! Now it seemed so impossible. The people's revolution! He wanted to be totally away from that sort of thing. Tonight he wanted to enjoy mingling with a totally different kind of people without feeling guilty about it, wanted to be in plush surroundings with a pretty woman on his arm and beautiful music playing in the background. If Liliana had been a part of it, he would have enjoyed being there with her, but Liliana *wasn't* a part of it and didn't want to be. She'd committed herself to another world. And he, too, was going to have to make some choices—just as she had told him.

He walked on along the quiet street past the Italian Embassy and the Japanese Embassy and the West German Embassy. A group of Japanese men in dark business suits was gathered in the entrance of a jewelry shop near the Mayan Hotel as the smartly dressed clerk displayed her wares. And in the clothing store next door, Hartley could see another Japanese man trying on a sports jacket. He stopped and looked at the window display, but before he turned away, he heard the voice of a clerk speaking perfect English from the doorway, "May I help you with a new suit today, sir?"

"No," Hartley said at first. "No, I don't...," and then he turned and looked directly at the clerk. "Do you sell tuxedos?"

It was crazy, he thought, even when he asked the question. Karen had assured him that he didn't need a tuxedo. But the clerk beckoned him to the rear of the store. "We have clothing for all occasions, sir," he said. And within thirty minutes, Hartley had handed over his American Express card. "The alterations can be complete in an hour," the clerk said. "Shall we bring it to your hotel?"

"No," Hartley said. "No. I'll be back. I'll wait in the Mayan bar or maybe the casino."

He found the casino closed and the bar dark and empty except for the bartender, but still, when he returned to pick up his tuxedo an hour later, he felt strangely excited, almost giddy, as the clerk laid the suit box in his arms. A tuxedo! He hadn't worn a tuxedo since college, and then he'd borrowed Brad's. He gripped the box under his arm and waved for a taxi. No more would he have to suffer his brother's left-handed compliments about his clothing.

He laughed. It was silly, he thought, all silly, but still it felt strangely good. He liked the man he had seen in the mirror when he tried the suit on, really liked him. He would feel right at home with corporate executives and diplomats and heads of state. And he had to laugh at himself again. But then, as his cab approached the center of the city just at dusk, he was suddenly brought back to the realities of Nicaragua. The entire plaza was bathed in floodlights, and armed soldiers were visible on every corner. In front of the National Theater, he could see flags of both the United States and Nicaragua waving side by side. And then the taxi was detoured down a back street by a military policeman who said the main streets had been closed to all but official vehicles until midnight. Karen wasn't kidding when she set about to mount a gala event.

He found a message to call her as soon as he got in, and when she answered, she was almost breathless, "Oh, I'm so glad you got me!" she said. "I was just leaving for the embassy. I'll meet you on the steps of the theater. They won't let you inside without a printed invitation, and I've got yours in my purse."

"Right," Hartley said. And suddenly, with the flow and excitement of her words, it was as though the events of the previous day with Liliana and the crisis at Agri-21 had never occurred. "I'll be waiting," he said.

It went without a hitch. He walked up the steps into the bright lights in front of the theater just as Karen broke away from the ambassador's party to meet him. "Hello," she called and then stopped in an instant of admiration. "You look wonderful!"

"And you," he said.

"I thought you didn't have a tuxedo."

"Surprise."

"Yes. And a nice one." She took his arm and led the way, handing both their invitations to the armed guard at the door and lowering her shawl to reveal her shoulders and the scooped neckline of her gown as they entered.

"Now I know the meaning of the word *stunning*," Hartley said when they took their seats.

"What?"

"You," he said over the din of the tuning orchestra. And he could actually feel the heightened rhythm of his heartbeat as he spoke. "You. Absolutely stunning."

"Oh, that's very nice," she said. "Thank you." She was about to say something more, but just then the orchestra was standing and the audience followed them, applauding as President Somoza entered his box and the orchestra played the Nicaraguan National Anthem. When it was over, the president waved and took his seat, and Ambassador Grubbs appeared in a spotlight on the stage accompanied by an interpreter.

"Keep your fingers crossed," Karen whispered.

But the ambassador functioned smoothly, "Mr. President, Honored Guests, this concert tonight is a gift from the American people to the Nicaraguan people. Just as the flags of both nations decorate this stage, this concert symbolizes the old and close friendship that exists between our two countries and our mutual support of democracy in the Western Hemisphere. It is a bond of friendship and support that we intend to keep alive for many years to come." His comments were followed by loud applause, and Grubbs remained on stage facing the flag with his hand over his heart while the orchestra played "The Star-Spangled Banner."

"Whew!" Karen whispered.

"Were you worried?"

"You haven't met him yet," Karen said. "I wrote that for him just an hour before we came here." She was about to say more, but as Ambassador Grubbs returned to his seat beside President Somoza, the house lights lowered and the concert began with Aaron Copland's "Appalachian Spring."

For Karen, it was a total triumph, and Ambassador Grubbs and his wife Ruby were the first to say so when Karen and Hartley entered the receiving line at the Kingston mansion two hours later. "Karen!" Mr. Grubbs said, "this is wonderful! And with stuff like we saw in the papers today, it couldn't have happened at a better time."

He hugged her around the shoulders, and Ruby cooed at her side in a South Carolina drawl, "Oh yes, yes, it's just wonderful to get all these musicians here." She turned and reached for Hartley's hand as she spoke. "Don't you think it was wonderful, Mr. Hartley? I do hope we can bring 'em here again real soon."

And for Hartley, too, it was no less a success from the moment they moved away from the Grubbses and Karen introduced him to Amanda Kingston. "Ronald Hartley? No. It can't be," Mrs. Kingston said. And she hugged him, too, as she turned to her husband in the line beside her. "Philip, this is Mortimer Hartley's son. Can you believe it? My goodness, I don't think you were more than twelve years old last time we saw you!"

Philip Kingston, standing next to the corpulent President Somoza, was tall and lean and easily the most commanding figure in the room. "Ronald, how good of you to be with us!" he said. "Delightful to see you after all this time. We were distressed when we heard of your father's death a few years back. He was a good friend—always kept in touch. I hope we can talk more later, but for now, I would like to introduce you to the President of the Republic."

"I can't believe it," Hartley said to Karen later. "Maybe you do this sort of thing all the time, but I never met a president before. I mean, only a short time ago, I was just a broke partner in a defunct airline."

Karen squeezed his arm. "Let me make a last check on our security and transportation arrangements, and then we can have some refreshments."

"I'll find the men's room," Hartley said.

As he moved up the wide central staircase past the armed guard and the golden cage of parrots on the landing, a string quartet was beginning to play a Strauss waltz in the great room below. But when he came out of the toilet two minutes later, the sound of music was being drowned by angry voices in the hallway, and he turned the corner to see Colonel Negroponte and Captain Segura standing almost nose to nose beside the telephone. "No," the Colonel was saying, "no, it shouldn't be allowed."

"But sir, I have this message from Father Molina...."

"Molina is a fool."

"Perhaps," Segura said. "Perhaps. I don't agree with his politics, but he was my teacher once, and I know he can be trusted. He says no rebels were involved."

"Everyone else believes rebels were involved."

"It was revenge," Segura said. "One man...."

"How do you know Molina's right?"

"He's a very reasonable man."

"Captain Segura, sometimes I begin to wonder about you. You know yourself—in all of this, there is only one important question: how does the Guardia respond to an attack? The identity of the attacker makes no difference. It looks like rebels staged an attack. People *believe* rebels staged an attack. The Guardia must respond to that attack. If we don't, we're inviting trouble."

"But if we prevent a peaceful demonstration...."

The colonel's voice was suddenly strident. "Captain, I do not want any demonstration to take place tomorrow."

"Yes sir," Segura said.

"Do you understand me?"

"Yes sir."

"No demonstrations."

Segura was about to say something more, but at that moment, the colonel saw Hartley, and his demeanor changed completely as he switched to English. "Ah, Mister Hartley!" He extended his hand. "We were just trying to decide how to solve these problems that have so troubled us at Agri-21. Have you met Captain Segura?"

"Yes," Hartley said. "We've met." For an instant, he locked eyes with Segura and then looked back at the colonel. "What *is* happening at Agri-21?"

"Don't you worry, Mr. Hartley. Police support has been increased. We have everything under control."

"My bank would certainly like to believe it."

"Oh yes. I assure you, all under control."

"How is Mrs. Kellner this evening?" Segura said.

"What? Oh, very well," Hartley said. "Excellent, in fact. She worked very hard for all this."

"I know," Segura said. "I worked with her."

"Oh. Of course. You must have. Congratulations."

Hartley left them there, feeling newly bothered by both Segura's tone and by what he had overheard concerning Agri-21. But a moment later, when he came down the steps and saw Karen standing beside the string quartet talking to Ambassador Grubbs in the great room, a sense of near intoxication swept all his other feelings aside.

She turned and waved, and by the time he reached the bottom of the grand stairs, she was waiting with outstretched hand. "Come," she said, "let's get a drink. I've hardly had time to talk to you all evening." She led him with moist fingers through the crowd. "I'm sorry things are so hectic, but officially, I'm still working."

"It's O.K.," he said. Ahead, he could see that Ambassador Grubbs was now talking to Daniél Cortez. "This is wonderful. Everybody I know in Nicaragua is here."

"Only the best," Karen said.

"Ah, Mr. Hartley," Cortez said. He reached for Hartley's hand and nodded toward Ambassador Grubbs. "I assume you've met your own ambassador."

"Oh yes."

"He's the lucky man who's with that good lookin' Karen Kellner tonight," Ambassador Grubbs said. He winked and blew a puff of blue cigar smoke into the air above their heads. "Oh, hello, Karen. I didn't see you standin' there." Grubbs laughed at his own joke and looked back at Cortez. "I have to watch myself with all these liberated women around," he said. He laughed again, this time winking directly at Karen and touching her arm as he turned back to Hartley and nodded toward Cortez. "How did you two guys get to know each other?"

"Mr. Hartley is one of our major business colleagues," Cortez said.

"Really?" Grubbs said. "Well I'm delighted to hear it. I don't know whether you realize it or not, Mr. Hartley, but if you're in business with Cortez here, you're workin' with one of the finest men in all Latin America."

"Oh, you are too kind," Cortez said.

"Not at all, not at all. Believe me, Hartley, I know what kind of trouble a man can get into in this part of the world. So take my word for it. You're very lucky." Grubbs turned back to Karen and again touched her arm, squeezing slightly as he nodded toward Hartley. "Have you given him the bad news yet?"

"No sir," Karen said, "not yet."

"Then you two had better run right over and get yourselves a drink, quick," Grubbs said.

"Yes sir, we will."

"What's he talking about?" Hartley said.

"Let's get a drink and I'll tell you," Karen said. They pushed on to the bar and then, with drinks in hand, she led him again to one side, away from the string quartet. "I'm sorry about this and it makes me mad as hell," she said, "but I've got to go back to work."

"What? When?"

"Right now. Mr. Grubbs wants me to write a press release for the morning edition of *El Tiempo*."

"Tonight?"

"Yes. It's this strike that's supposed to take place tomorrow. Grubbs wants to make it clear that the United States stands firmly behind President Somoza. Kind of a warning to any rebels who might get ideas."

"Then our date is already over."

"Ron, I'm sorry. Mr. Cárdenas the publisher is here, and he's already called his editor to leave space."

"Doesn't anything in this part of the world go as planned?"

"Believe me, I hate it as much as you do."

"I could go with you, wait till you finish."

"I can't work that way. Besides, I've got to do different versions for all the papers. By the time I finish, it'll be morning."

"Damn!"

"Rick Adams is going to take me to the office now. You can ride in with us or I can arrange for you to ride with someone else."

"No, wait," Hartley said. He felt a sudden flash of heat behind his eyes. "Why should Rick Adams take you?"

"He's driving an embassy car."

"Why don't *you* take the embassy car and I'll go with you. Let Rick arrange a ride with someone else."

"Ron, it's official business and it's better this way. Please try to understand."

"Sometimes I get tired of understanding."

She put her hand on his arm. "I'll call you tomorrow. Believe me, I want to see you, spend some time without all the interruptions. We can have dinner—just the two of us—when the pressure's off."

"Yes. I'd like that," Hartley said. "Really I would.

28

Segura watched them leave. All evening he had been planning to corner Karen for at least a moment of conversation, but his argument with Colonel Negroponte had distracted him, and now he saw that it was too late. He watched her walk down the front steps with Rick Adams on one side and Hartley on the other, and suddenly he felt that all life had gone out of the evening. It was a feeling that troubled him immensely. This was the kind of party that every Guardia officer longed to attend. The President, the top brass, the heads of industry, the representatives of foreign governments, all were there in the company of beautiful and interesting women. But tonight, between his conflict with his own superior and the coldness of this North American woman, it had all gone sour.

What did it mean? he wondered. This Gringa with the wonderful body. He had admired American women before, but this one! So beautiful, but turning on and off like a faucet. One minute despising him, another minute inviting him into her home for sherry and letting him kiss her, and the next minute acting as though none of it had happened and working with him like a man to plan security for the concert. The whole business left him with a kind of dull ache in his chest. It was ridiculous, he thought, to be so subject to the whims of a woman. And then there was Colonel Negroponte.

He shrugged and went indoors to check his men. Perhaps the party would revive as the night went on. But with Karen gone, he found himself totally preoccupied by thoughts of the threatened strike and his argument with the colonel. And as soon as the president left with his military escort thirty minutes later, Segura turned things over to his lieutenant, bid goodnight to Amanda Kingston, and walked to his car.

"Take me to Baná," he said to the driver.

"Baná, sir?"

"Yes. To the cathedral."

"The cathedral?"

"Am I not speaking clearly?" Segura said.

"Oh, yes sir," the driver said. "Just—well, Baná is pretty dead this time of night."

"I promise you I'm not looking for excitement."

They moved on alone across the bare countryside until they entered the dimly lighted town, moving slowly block by block beneath the single bulbs at the corners of the streets until they reached the cathedral rising darkly at the center. "Go around to the residence hall where the priests live," Segura said. There were no lights on the cathedral grounds, and for a moment after the driver stopped, Segura sat and let his eyes adjust until he could clearly see the doorways of the separate apartments. "That one. Over there." He pointed across the driver's shoulder. "That's where I'll be." He found his pistol belt on the dark seat and strapped it around his waist. "I'll be back."

It had been years since he had entered that door, but the musty smell inside the hall made him feel almost like a schoolboy, and even in the dark, he found the second door on the right with no trouble at all. He knocked. "Father Antonio." His voice cracked and he cleared his throat as he knocked again. "Father Molina!"

This time he heard Molina calling back. "Who is it?"

"An old student."

"My God, do you know what time it is?!"

"Yes, Father. Open the door."

And a moment later Molina stood in the doorway with the light at his back forming a kind of halo through his tousled white hair. "Who is it?" he said again and then stopped as he saw the glint of brass on the Guardia uniform. "Oh my God!"

163

"It's Raúl Segura, Father."

Molina's hands dropped to his sides in total defenselessness. "Raúl, so, now at last you've come to take me."

"I'm alone, Father," Segura said. "And I didn't come to take you anywhere." For a moment, the two men stood silently in the doorway. "May I come in?"

"You're wearing the pistol. There's no way I can stop you."

"I didn't know who else might be here," Segura said. He unsnapped the pistol belt and laid it on the table beside the door. "Now may I come in?"

"Raúl Segura, you make me weep," Molina said. He shook his head in dismay and turned as Segura followed him into the apartment. "Am I under arrest?"

"No, Father."

"Usually, a midnight visit from the Guardia means arrest...."

"I came to warn you."

"Why would you want to warn me?"

"Father...."

"You didn't bother to warn the others."

"Father, please listen. I know you've been working with the unions. But the government is not going to allow your strike."

"Strikes are perfectly legal in this country."

"But not this one," Segura said. "We have evidence that the unions are filled with Marxist rebels from the Sandinista Front. And after the killings this week, we will consider any public demonstration as an act of rebellion against the constitutional government. The president has declared a *state of siege*."

"Then what recourse do people have when the government assaults them?"

"The courts—as always."

"Did you come here at midnight to make a joke?"

"No, Father. And I didn't come to argue. I'm giving you information. After the killings this week...."

"I told you what that was," Molina said. "On the telephone. There was no rebel involved. It was entirely one man...."

"If you mean Quetoda, we know that he was also working with

the unions—with Rubio—with the whole...."

"Only one man using the gun that was taken when Guardia men—your men—killed two campesinos and then murdered his wife."

"I do not agree that Guardia men did anything."

"Raúl, you know the truth as well as I. Whether it was Guardia men or hired civilians. Those were approved executions!"

"Father, it makes no difference now!"

"It makes all the difference in the world."

"Just listen to me! I've been ordered to stop your demonstration—to do whatever is necessary. Please call it off."

"Why do you bother?" Molina said. His voice was calm now, almost pensive.

"Because I don't want my men to shoot you."

"Then you haven't lost it all, have you?"

"What?"

"All my teaching. You haven't lost it all. You still care about something."

"Father...."

"Oh, you're working very hard to stamp it out. I can see that. Working hard to replace your mortal soul with power and greed and lust and the approval of corrupt men! And you'll succeed, I'm sure, if you keep on the way you're going. But you were one of my very best pupils, Raúl, and it's gratifying to see that some remnant of young Raúl Segura still lives inside that despised uniform!"

"Is this the thanks I get for trying to save your life?"

"Thanks!? You come to threaten me at midnight and expect *thanks*?!"

"So be it," Segura said.

"You're a hired assassin!"

Segura moved toward the door and then turned angrily back. "So be it," he said again. "I've done what I came to do. I have my orders and you know the score. But you will not be the only man in that demonstration tomorrow, and if you lead the others to their death, you will be more guilty than I."

"No!" Molina said. "No." His voice was loud now. "Don't try

165

to smear the guilt on me! If you pull a single trigger tomorrow morning, *you* will be guilty of murder. *You* and all those who follow you. Guilty of murdering unarmed campesinos. You know they're not Marxist rebels as well as I do, and if you kill one of them there's no way you can escape the damnation of God for your crime!"

"I have my orders."

"Must you obey them?"

"I am an officer of the Guardia."

"Then you've traded your manhood for a pistol!"

Segura's open hand flashed out, slapping backward across Molina's cheek and jerking his head painfully to one side.

"Now you must feel better," Molina said.

Segura's hand was cocked to strike again, but he stopped as Molina looked up with blood in the corner of his mouth.

"I'm sure all boys want to hit their teacher sometime."

And without speaking again, Segura rushed out into the darkness.

For a moment Molina closed his eyes in a wave of dizziness. But when he opened them again, he found himself looking directly at the pistol Segura had left on the table beside the door, and even against the stinging pain of his cheek, he had to smile. He took the gun and moved quickly through the dark hall, arriving at the front door just as the headlights of Segura's car flashed full in his face. "Raúl," he called. "Raúl...." He waved the pistol in the air, and his speech was slurred through his swollen lip as he handed the gun through the open window of the car. "You forgot your manhood," he said. "I thought you might need it in the morning."

29

Just after sunrise, Hartley woke from a dream of an American staging area south of Hue. In the dream, strange tanks and troop carriers were moving in to protect his airfield, but instead of protecting the planes, the tanks were bumping into them and crushing their wings, and Hartley woke himself up yelling at the tank commanders to watch what they were doing.

In an instant, sitting suddenly upright in the elegant hotel room, he realized where he was, and he had to laugh. Sunlight was angling in across the plaza and reflecting golden from the mirror on the opposite wall. But then he realized that the sound of armor had not all been in his dream. He could still hear it. He kicked off the sheet and went to the window, and there across the plaza, he could see two World War II Sherman tanks grinding into position before each wing of the Palacio Nacional. Troop carriers were following the tanks, and Guardia soldiers in full combat gear were assembling barrier lines with saw horses and ropes across nearby streets. "Jesus!" Hartley whispered. "Looks like they mean business."

He dressed and went downstairs to find a paper and see if anybody knew what was going on. Maybe he could find Karen's news release, he thought. But there were no papers in the lobby, and as he started out to the street, he felt the hand of the hotel watchman suddenly firm on his arm at the door. "Excuse me, sir. We're asking all guests to remain inside today. The streets may be dangerous."

"I'm going for a paper."

"Yes, sir. But...."

Hartley pulled away. "I'll be right back. Believe me."

The man let him go, but he had to walk two blocks before he found a copy of *El Tiempo* and there, on the crowded front page, he found the partial answer to his questions in the headline: "STATE OF SIEGE DECLARED." And he had to read the story even before he paid for the paper. President Somoza had declared martial law and suspended all constitutional rights, especially the right to assemble or organize political groups, it said. And then, just beneath that story, he found the piece that Karen must have written: "A Vote of Confidence from the U.S."

"In an interview late last night, U.S. Ambassador Dan Grubbs expressed deep concern at the recent killings which have grown out of labor disputes in Nicaragua.

"'Evidence suggests that this violence was inspired by Marxist agitators,' Grubbs said. 'And I want to go on record condemning such violence. President Somoza and the government of Nicaragua have worked hard to correct labor abuses, and they deserve the confidence of the Nicaraguan people.'

"Ambassador Grubbs spoke strongly in his condemnation of communist Sandinista insurgents. 'There is no place for communists on the American mainland,' he said. 'And let there be no doubt that we pledge anew our unqualified support for President Somoza and the government of Nicaragua in their efforts to maintain the principles of free enterprise and democracy in this wonderful emerging country.'"

There was more, but Hartley only scanned the rest. Karen had done well, he thought. She was extremely efficient. But something about the whole thing bothered him. It was hard to think of either Liliana Summerfield or any of those underpaid workers as Marxist agitators. And then for a moment, as he folded the paper and walked back to the hotel for breakfast, he had a picture of Karen in her low cut evening gown writing the ambassador's official declaration of policy in the form of an interview while the ambassador himself was still at a party miles away. What was going on? he wondered.

But his thoughts were interrupted by sudden troop activity in the shadow of the ruined cathedral on the opposite side of the plaza. The tanks were now firmly in place with their .90 millimeter rifles aimed down the approach avenues, and he could see snipers taking up positions on the roofs and in the windows of government buildings. "State of Siege," the paper had called the situation. That declaration allowed the government to do virtually anything, and clearly they were ready to do it.

By the time he got back to his room, he could hear music playing from somewhere, and when he looked from his window he could see a column of civilian marchers assembling east of the plaza. Both the flag of Nicaragua and the red and black flag of the Farmers' Syndicate waved above their heads, and behind the flags, he could see signs and banners with painted slogans: "Nicaragua for ALL people." "Enforce Land Reform Laws." "Increase Minimum Wages." "Protect the Rights of Workers." All pretty non-threatening stuff, he thought.

But then, as the marchers moved from the avenue into the east side of the plaza, he saw a helmeted company of Guardia soldiers move forward to meet them from the opposite side. It was clearly a company prepared for combat—not crowd control. There were no shields, no dogs, no water hoses. Only billy clubs, rifles, and bayonets.

Gradually, the two groups converged and for a moment stopped face to face in front of the hotel so that Hartley could see them quite clearly beyond the venenera flowers in the Cruz de Cristo tree as the Guardia officer raised his megaphone and addressed the marchers just as Segura had done on the night at the theater. It might even be Segura now, Hartley thought. At that distance, he couldn't tell for sure, but he could hear the officer's harangue delivered point blank at the leader of the march—obviously a priest—who was standing just a few feet in front of him: "This march is illegal and you are ordered to disband and disperse."

The priest gave some reply, which Hartley could not hear, and without further hesitation, the column of demonstrators moved forward directly toward the rank of soldiers. The last command

Hartley heard was, "Fix bayonets!" And then the plaza erupted.

In all his combat time in the Far East, Hartley had never actually seen anyone bayoneted. But on that morning, he saw it in the central plaza of Managua in clear sunlight and beneath cloudless skies, the demonstrators attempting to move around the company of soldiers and the soldiers simply fanning out and stopping them with cold steel, using the standard butt stroke, cross, parry, and thrust that Hartley himself had been taught in basic infantry training.

The first man to go down was the one carrying the sign saying, "Enforce Land Reform Laws," who tried for all of three seconds to defend himself with the shaft of his sign. He managed to delay his attacker, but he was no match for the soldier, who easily parried the sign, slammed the butt of his rifle against the marcher's head, and then rammed his bayonet fully into the man's chest as the company exploded forward, slamming and thrusting, slamming and thrusting beneath an umbrella of gunfire from the roof tops. By this time, the demonstrators were running for cover, pursued by soldiers who pulled them down and prodded them with bayonets or beat them with billy clubs and then left them for the roundup crew, who trussed them like steers and threw them into waiting army trucks to be hauled away.

"Jesus!" Hartley said. "Oh Jesus!" It was the only thing he could say. He was kneeling beside the open window making as small a target as possible, but he could not stop watching. His mouth was dry, and on the concrete apron of the plaza near the fountain, he could see bodies lying like empty grain sacks that no one seemed concerned about at all. "Oh Jesus!" he said again. And then he realized the telephone was ringing behind him.

It was Karen, slightly breathless, and with the noise in the street he could hardly hear her. "Ron, what's happening over there? We heard gunfire."

"Gunfire! Yes!" He was shouting into the phone but he couldn't stop. "It's a rout! A massacre!"

"Wait a minute. Rick Adams wants to talk to you."

Below the window somebody opened up with a shotgun, and

Hartley ducked down just as Rick started. "The streets are blocked and we can't get over there," Rick said. "Can you tell me what's happening?"

Hartley rose up again to look over the window ledge. "There're snipers on the roof, troops in the streets bayoneting people, arresting people. I can count maybe a dozen bodies on the ground. Two of 'em women!" And then suddenly he was shouting again as a wave of rage washed over him, "The Guardia has just slaughtered a bunch of unarmed demonstrators! They're murderers! They're animals! They don't deserve to exist outside of cages!"

But Rick was suddenly gone and Karen was back on the line. "They're slaughtering unarmed people!" he said again, "absolutely unarmed people!"

"I'm worried about you," Karen said. "The embassy is open to any American in danger. But there's no way we can come get you."

"It's O.K."

"Come here if you can get here."

"Thanks, but...."

"We're trying to size things up, see what needs to be done."

"I'll sit tight," Hartley said. "Believe me, the street is nowhere to be."

But it was all over in an hour. By early evening the tanks were gone, and except for armed troops who continued patrolling in groups of three or four, the streets seemed almost normal. Hartley found the evening papers and sat in the hotel lobby to watch the strangely sterilized television reports which called the shooting "a Guardia defeat of communist agitators," without once mentioning the number of civilian dead. Even the onsite television film showed no close-ups of bodies and no pictures of any violent actions committed by any soldier, making the whole business seem strangely benign compared to what Hartley had actually seen.

But it was a short article on the second page of *La Prensa* that interested him most: "Rebel Force Attacks Jinotega." The article was so small, he almost missed it, but he quickly went back and took a second look. "At noon today, fighters of the Sandinista Liberation Front staged an all-out attack against the Guardia barracks at Jinotega," it said.

"According to anonymous telephone calls, the assault was in retaliation for the Guardia action against the demonstrators in Managua. At last report, twenty Guardia soldiers had been killed and the outpost was left in flames as rebels withdrew into the jungle carrying with them an unknown number of their dead and wounded. 'This is the beginning,' a rebel spokesman said on the telephone. 'No longer can the people of Nicaragua tolerate the brutality of the Somoza government.' Colonel Carlos Negroponte, Guardia Chief of Staff, promised a quick and punishing response."

"God Almighty damn!" Hartley whispered. He read the article again, and then he had to stand and move around the lobby. "God Almighty!" They were probably using the ammunition he had flown to Jinotega. He wondered if Liliana was anywhere near the fighting. "Oh God!" He was standing at the center of the lobby now, looking into the glittering eye of the macaw in the bird cage. "It's really started," he whispered. What would it do to the investment at Agri-21? What would happen to the tractors when they got here? And then, with a sudden sense of shame, he remembered the two women demonstrators whose bodies had been left like sacks on the concrete plaza that morning. "Oh Jesus," he said. "Oh Jesus!"

30

Molina was saved by his cross. He had stepped forward defiantly toward the bayonets that waited in the plaza, but the young soldier who stopped him had been nervous, swinging his rifle wildly toward Molina's head and knocking him down but then freezing in stark panic and running away when he saw the silver cross on his chest.

For hours afterward, Molina was barely conscious, lying with eighteen other men on the floor of a cell in El Castillo prison, but by the next morning his head was almost clear and, at the sound of voices in the corridor, he looked up through the dim light to see Segura and two sergeants at the door. "That one," Segura said, "the priest. Clean him up and bring him to me."

"These other men need medical help," Molina said.

But Segura only gestured to the sergeants in response, and barely twenty minutes later, Molina was standing before the desk in the captain's office like a schoolboy waiting for the headmaster to recognize him.

"I'm surprised you're alive," Segura said. "Some of these men would welcome a chance to skewer a priest."

"You are reprehensible," Molina said.

"I'll admit things went further than I'd planned."

"Tell that to the widows and orphans you created yesterday."

"Don't lecture me, Father. It's my turn now." Segura lit a cigarette and walked around from behind the desk, now looking hard into Molina's eyes. "Do you know what you did yesterday?"

he said. "In addition to pushing twelve men and women to their deaths? Do you? By breaking the law, by defying my request?" He sat back against the edge of the desk. "You put the country under martial law, that's what you did. Yes. You. State of siege. Instead of making the country more open and free, you locked it up. Yesterday, a group could get together and discuss their problems. Today, if I see more than three people together, I'll arrest them. I will. I'll throw them into that cell with you and the others so they can express their appreciation." Segura looked away toward the window and pulled on his cigarette. "Why was Rubio not with you?"

"Rubio had no business with us," Molina said.

"Did he send the message to Jinotega?"

"I don't know what you mean."

"No, of course you don't. Priests are innocent to the ways of the world, aren't they?"

"I have been barely conscious for...."

"And of course you didn't know the rebels planned to attack Jinotega if your demonstration went badly."

"No. What attack at Jinotega?"

"Lies come awkwardly from the mouth of a priest. Did Rubio lead it?"

"Why all this interest in Rubio? He's a crippled poet. A playwright."

"And what else is he?" Segura said. "What else is he besides a crippled poet?" Molina shrugged, and Segura blew a large puff of smoke across his face. "One of your devoted students, no? A student and a poet. Wonderful! A devotee of the great Molina, with his girlish face and his crippled leg. And an Uzzi submachine gun across his back! What else?"

"I don't know what you want."

"I'll tell you what I want," Segura said. "I want you to tell me the truth. Rubio is the most international figure among you—even more than you. He has contacts in every country in Latin America. We know that. And we also know who's running this show. Rubio and Castillo. And those others—Fonseca and Borge, hiding so neatly and giving orders just over the Honduran border. The Americans found this out through their CIA." For a moment, he smoked silently, looking out of the window. "Rubio is the one who can arrange for arms, isn't he?"

"I don't know what you're talking about."

"You should have been a lawyer, Father. *Arms!* I'm talking about arms! Rifles. Bullets. Machine guns. Grenades!" His voice was loud now as he moved close into Molina's face. "While you pushed twelve people to their deaths yesterday, Rubio attacked Jinotega. Rubio had procured arms for the rebels. Through Cuba, through the Dominican Republic, through Panama. Arms to overthrow your government. How did he get them into the country? Who were his contacts? Where did he buy them?"

"I have no idea. I counseled against the use of arms every time it came up."

"So you have discussed it with him?"

"I advocated nonviolence from the beginning."

"You are a saint."

"I had no arms. *We* had no arms. And after yesterday, I think I also have no government worthy of the name, either. May I sit?"

"No," Segura said. "I'm going to release you."

"Release me?"

"How could I imprison a saint? Especially one who pants so eagerly after martyrdom?"

"You are the most cynical man I know."

"How could I imprison Antonio Molina, the poet—my old teacher?"

"I don't want your special favors."

"Oh, don't fool yourself, Father. This is no favor, believe me. Unless it's a favor to us. This is hard nosed politics. The Pope would be complaining about us to every government in the world, if we imprisoned poor Father Antonio. Everybody can see that you're obviously the innocent dupe of communist conspirators. But you're still Antonio Molina the Poet, and you're much less trouble to us free and babbling nonsense out there in the street than you would be here in prison. Besides, your cathedral school needs supervision. We'd hate to interfere with the education of future scholars and poets."

"What are you trying to do?"

Segura turned and called into the outer office, "Lieutenant Valen, find a car to take Father Molina back to Baná."

"To Baná, sir?"

"Yes. Let's take him home. Just like a schoolboy, he was lured into trouble by bad companions, but I think he's repented now." Segura walked through the door into the next room, and the lieutenant stood as the captain leaned forward to whisper close to his ear, "And assign someone to watch his every move," Segura said. "He may be our most valuable source of intelligence."

31

The attack on Jinotega became the major news story of the following day, and by morning, newspapers were competing with each other for flamboyant headlines: "Major Rebel Attack," "Guardia Outpost in flames," "State of Siege!" And one paper filled the top third of its front page with the single word: "WAR!"

Hartley bought them all as he returned from breakfast, and then as he reached his hotel room, his telephone began to ring. First, it was his mother who had seen the news on television and was worried sick about his safety. Was he all right? she wanted to know. And a few minutes later, it was Brad who, although he asked after Hartley's health, was worried sick about their investments and the safety of the tractors. Hartley calmed them as best he could. "We've got no reason to worry yet," he told Brad, "but I'll be checking. We'll know more in a couple of days."

And then it was Cortez, calling directly without the aid of his secretary. "Mr. Hartley, could we talk today? Perhaps lunch. I'll pick you up."

"You think it's safe now?"

"Yes."

"The news reports sound terrible."

"Believe me. I am a cautious man."

They went again to the Mayan Hotel, this time with less fanfare than before but with more military presence, an extra armed guard beside the driver in Cortez's limo and quadrupled protection around the hotel itself.

Otherwise, the world of Cortez and the Mayan Hotel seemed oblivious to the national crisis. The casino was just opening for the afternoon, and Oriana spotted them passing the doorway. "Daniél," she said, "are things so bad? Will you never come to see me again?"

"Never fear, my pet," Cortez said. He kissed her cheek and smiled broadly. "When things let up, I'll be back. Never doubt it. Why don't you come join us for dessert, in a while."

"Yes. Nice. I'd like that," Oriana said.

"Good." Cortez watched her walk away. "Lovely," he said softly. "Lovely. Don't you think so, Mr. Hartley? Truly one of God's gifts. Sometimes I almost wish I were not a married man." He smiled broadly again and gestured toward the restaurant. But as soon as he was seated across the table from Hartley, his smile faded completely. "What I have to say is very delicate," Cortez said. "I hope you will understand."

"Are there more problems at Agri-21?"

"No, no. Not at Agri-21. Not this time."

"You know your tractors should arrive at the port of El Paisello any day?"

"Yes. We're ready for them."

"Good."

"Everything for the moment is calm at Agri-21. But I want to talk about ways to keep it calm. 'Insurance,' you might call it."

"What kind of insurance?"

Cortez swallowed his bite of bread, and when he leaned forward across the table, Hartley noticed a small white crumb caught in the corner of his mustache. "As you know from the newspapers, the government has been attacked by rebel forces who call themselves the 'Sandinista Front.'"

"I'm not in the least surprised," Hartley said.

"What?!"

"From the Guardia's action yesterday...."

"Oh...."

"...I'm surprised it hasn't happened sooner."

"That was bad business," Cortez said. "I'll admit it. Unfortunate in every way."

"They shot and bayoneted unarmed demonstrators."

"Mr. Hartley, that demonstration was a flagrant violation of the laws of Nicaragua. It was a test of the government's will to maintain order. And I promise you...."

"How many dead?" Hartley interrupted.

"Please, Mr. Hartley. Understand. We are faced by an insidious enemy."

"How many dead?"

"Do you think the Sandinistas will hesitate to sacrifice a few lives if it will win them a victory of public opinion?"

"I don't understand," Hartley said.

"Listen," Cortez said. "Listen. I'll give you a scenario. The rebels, the Marxists, appeal to a 'higher good' and send ignorant peasants illegally against a resolute police force. A few peasants are killed. The world cries 'brutality' and hates our government. Then the rebels attack us, claiming to be democratic heroes trying to overthrow a dictator, and the world applauds them—even sends them money and weapons!"

"Are you saying the rebels won yesterday?"

"Yes! That's exactly what I'm saying. They won big, Mr. Hartley, as you say in the States—they won very big. Here in the city, they won the propaganda battle, and so far as world opinion goes, that can prove to be a very great victory, indeed. But there, out there in the field at our outposts, they won in a different way, and that is what worries us most."

"Would've been better to just let the farmers demonstrate, wouldn't it?" Hartley said.

"Yes. Now, I suppose, with hindsight, it looks that way. But the government could not possibly win yesterday. No matter what it did, it could not win. We had two bad choices: either to be weak and give in to law violators or to be strong and resist. We believe that in the end, victory will go to the strong."

"I see."

Cortez leaned again across the table. "What surprised us most was the equipment and training of the rebel forces at Jinotega. They overran the Guardia troops in minutes."

"Why are you telling me all this?'

"It is necessary for you to understand, Mr. Hartley. International business does not occur in a political vacuum."

"No, of course not. But...."

"You are our valued associate. We think you can help enormously."

"Me?"

"It's really very simple. Under President Johnson, your government suspended shipment of arms to Nicaragua until the land reform problem was corrected. But now, even though we have a good land reform law, the U.S. has not resumed the arms shipments."

"I thought the strike yesterday was largely *about* land reform," Hartley said.

"That was all propaganda," Cortez said. "Don't you see? Marxist propaganda. An effort to open old wounds. Oh, we'll admit that things have not been perfect. Nothing ever is. Bureaucracies make mistakes, after all. But I tell you, Mr. Hartley, Nicaragua has made great strides. We're more democratic now than ever in our history."

"What is it you want me to do?"

"Help us regain U.S. support."

"How can I do that? I have no political power."

"You may have more than you think."

"And besides, I thought Mr. Grubbs gave you support in his speech at the concert," Hartley said, "and in the newspaper."

"Oh, we are very grateful for his kind words, Mr. Hartley. Yes indeed. Words are wonderful, but...." Cortez rubbed his fingers together like a merchant testing new material. "We need the hard stuff—more modern rifles, rocket launchers, combat helicopters."

"Aren't your diplomatic people requesting all this?"

"Yes. But understand. Many nations ask the U.S. for aid. Your government may hear us and they may not. But if the appeal comes from U.S. citizens—like yourself—who have invested American capital with the hope of bringing new money to the States—then I think your government is more inclined to take whatever action is necessary to protect U.S. interests." Cortez smiled for the first time since the beginning of the conversation. "Seen that way, I promise you that your voice carries much more weight than even the voice of President Somoza himself."

"Let me get this straight," Hartley said. "You want me to go to Ambassador Grubbs and ask him to request more military aid from Washington?"

"That would be a good beginning, yes."

"To protect Agri-21?"

"No. To protect American investment in Nicaragua."

"I don't like it at all."

"Let's not deceive ourselves, Mr. Hartley. We're talking about survival. We must use whatever we have. You know Ambassador Grubbs. And I couldn't help noticing at the Kingstons' party—you also have another very attractive connection at the embassy."

"I find the whole idea totally unacceptable," Hartley said.

"Of course, I can understand your reluctance—especially if you're emotionally involved with the young woman...."

"No," Hartley interrupted. "It's not that. It's the idea of asking for U.S. arms, maybe even U.S. troops, to protect *your* farm."

"It's your farm, too, Mr. Hartley—at least until we fully repay your millions. I'm sure you want to protect the interests of your bank."

"Jesus!"

"Is it such a bad thing to defend your property?" For a moment Hartley had no answer, and Cortez was again leaning across the table. "But it's not just *our* farm," Cortez said. "Our farm is only one part. The job is to protect the entire country of Nicaragua— even the whole of Central America—from communist attack."

"How can you call it 'communist attack?' These are campesinos asking for the laws to be enforced."

"But they're backed by hardcore Marxist leaders. These guerillas are real, Mr. Hartley. They're all around us. They're in the jungles, they're in the mountains. They're supported by the Cubans and the

Russians, and now it seems they're far better trained and supplied than we suspected."

"I thought you had such a crack Guardia force."

"Maybe we've been deluded," Cortez said. "But of course, so far, the Guardia has only been used for police work. It hasn't really been tested."

"Or maybe it only performs well against unarmed civilians."

Cortez sat upright against the back of his chair, and small white crescents appeared suddenly beneath his eyes. "Mr. Hartley, I can see that you do not like the Guardia, and I will admit that in the last few days their performance has left much to be desired. But that only proves my point. The Guardia must be improved. We need renewed U.S. help in order to do it. If we fail, you'll find the troops of Fidel Castro camping in the fields of Agri-21 and maybe farther north before he's through. Millions in U.S. investment will be lost. And all for lack of help from Washington."

"Is it really Washington's business?"

"Only if you think protecting U.S. life, property, and investment is Washington's business."

"Jesus, help us!" Hartley said again.

"Jesus is fine as far as He goes," Cortez said. "But I think war with the rebels will require something stronger."

Hartley did not smile. Suddenly he wanted to be somewhere else, out, anywhere away from Cortez. But he realized that Oriana had entered the room, and he stood as she came toward their table.

"Ah, my beautiful, come sit down," Cortez said. "Cheer us up. Our friend Ronald has become upset at the actions of the Guardia."

"Oh?"

"Yes. Very upset." He stopped and ordered dessert from the waiter who hovered above Oriana's shoulder. "Oriana, tell him that the Guardia is not all bad, that all members are not monsters."

"Oh, no indeed," Oriana said. "They come from the best families in Nicaragua. I'm speaking of the officers, of course. Daniél is a colonel in the reserves, aren't you, Daniél?"

"Yes. That's right."

Hartley only smiled, but in the moment of silence, he was aware of Oriana's perfume, like the scent of some exotic night flower from across the table. "Oh," she continued, "as with anything, you find a bad one now and then, but in my experience—most have been perfect gentlemen."

"I think Mr. Hartley has been working too hard," Cortez said. The crumb was gone from his mustache, and suddenly he was cordial again, leaning forward and smiling. "I mean, Ronald, you've done a great deal since coming to Nicaragua. You need a vacation."

"I was thinking of going back to the States."

"Not because of politics, I hope," Oriana said. She laid her hand on his wrist in a gesture of restraint. "Because, listen, Mr. Hartley—may I call you Ronald?"

"Ron."

She smiled. "Ron, listen. Politics in Nicaragua is like the rumbling of an old volcano. Every now and then it roars and shakes and sends up a small puff of smoke—but then, nothing—everything is calm—nothing for a year, ten years, maybe longer before it rumbles again and sends up another puff of smoke."

"But it could blow," Hartley said.

"Oh yes. Just as lightning could strike. So wise people do not build houses atop volcanoes or go out in thunderstorms." Oriana laughed. "But nothing ever really changes here. You will see, if you stay long enough. It really means nothing at all."

"You should be in politics," Cortez said.

Oriana laughed and shook her head as she slipped her spoon into the chocolate mousse the waiter had set before her. "I'm one who doesn't like to build on top of volcanoes," she said.

"Have you been to Mariposa lately?" Cortez said.

"No. And I've missed it."

"She has a beautiful villa that I persuaded her to buy near mine on the island of Mariposa," Cortez said to Hartley, "a villa looking over the cliff to the sea."

"I must go there soon before the rainy season begins," Oriana said. "Have you never seen our offshore islands, Mr. Hartley?"

"No, I'm afraid not."

"Oh, you must see them!"

"Yes."

"They're paradise."

"One trip to Mariposa," Cortez said, "and I tell you, Mr. Hartley, you'll be hooked forever—mangoes, papayas, bananas, bread fruit, flowers cascading down the hills, game that lives wild in the forests and waterways."

"Sounds lovely."

"I will be going there soon," Oriana said. "Perhaps you could bring him out for a visit, Daniél. Or maybe you could come on your own, Ron, come and stay with me if Daniél can't get away."

"Wonderful idea," Cortez said. "Let me look into it. I'll see what I can arrange."

They left Oriana smiling at the door of the casino thirty minutes later. But with all their talk of paradise on Mariposa, Cortez did not remain long away from the subject of political influence. Seated in the air-conditioned limo, he settled back, reached beneath the lapel of his jacket, and then rearranged the bulge of his coat as he withdrew a typed list of names and telephone numbers. "What you finally decide to do, of course, is your business," he said to Hartley. "But this list of congressmen and senators might be of help."

"Congressmen and senators?"

"Yes. And corporation presidents." Cortez placed the document in Hartley's hand and leaned back as he continued. "Now," he said, "going to Ambassador Grubbs is important. It must be done, and I think you will find a sympathetic ear there. But more important ultimately are the voices and votes of senators and members of Congress. You'll recognize your own representatives on that list, of course. But I've taken the liberty of underscoring the names of key committee members—the foreign relations committee, the armed services committee, the committees on international trade, money and banking, fair trade practices. Others."

Hartley sat back in the corner of the limousine and looked at Cortez in disbelief as they wound through the twisting streets, and even in the cool of the air conditioning, his scalp prickled as though from needles of heat rash.

"I have also underlined the names of those who have previously shown interest," Cortez continued. "Senator Gerard on the trade committee, for example, is a brother of Amanda Kingston here at American Fruit Company. Senator Kepler, on the armed services committee, has long believed that the U.S. should have a permanent airbase in Nicaragua—such as the one that was used to launch that unfortunate Bay of Pigs invasion."

"Wait," Hartley said. "Wait." Cortez looked at him quizzically. "You're asking me to become a lobbyist for Nicaragua!"

"No, Ronald, no. Not at all. I'm asking you to become a lobbyist for First International Bank. I'm asking you to lobby for the preservation of democracy and the freedom of American corporations to invest and profit from business in a secure and peaceful country. Certainly Washington is sensitive to that."

"All this is very new to me," Hartley said.

"It's really very simple," Cortez said. "Get your government to send us arms so we can protect your business interests. In El Salvador, the aid came too late and U.S. corporations are pulling out, losing millions because of the war. We don't want it to happen here."

"No," Hartley said. "No, certainly."

"Appeal to your representatives. Get your bank to make the appeal."

"Suppose I don't," Hartley said. "Or suppose Washington doesn't give you the arms."

"Then—then I'm afraid that the one million two hundred thousand dollars you lent us might just as profitably have been dropped into Ocotal volcano."

For a long moment, Hartley did not answer. They were entering the central city now, passing through the Mercado as they approached the plaza where the streets that had been desolate the previous day were now crowded with people. "See, it is just as Oriana told you," Cortez said. "Nicaraguans have a short memory for catastrophe. They're like children. A rumble here, a tremor there, a puff of smoke, and life goes on as usual."

"Would their memory be so short if there were no Guardia to correct their thinking?" Hartley said.

"Ronald, what are we going to do with you?"

"Just answer my question."

"My friend, I admire your democratic ideals. They are fine for North America. But here we have a different story. I know the Nicaraguan people. And believe me, those ideals can never work in Nicaragua during our lifetime."

"Saying that just ensures it."

"I know what I see," Cortez said, "and everywhere there is proof that God in His wisdom did not really create people equal, in spite of what Thomas Jefferson may have said. Many of our people are still in the Stone Age, for example. And beyond that, the rest of us are an unreliable mix. Some are strong, some are weak; some are brilliant, some are stupid. A very few are ambitious, and almost all are greedy and slothful. But I am not responsible for all those others. I am responsible only for myself. And I know that if I do not design the world to suit myself, I will be forced to live in a world designed by others to suit someone else. And to me, that would be intolerable."

They were approaching the hotel now, and Hartley reached for the door latch as the limo stopped in front of the columned portico. "The lunch was very informative," he said.

"Think about it," Cortez said. He pointed to the folded list of legislators in Hartley's hand. "We can act or we can wait for others to act. But believe me, if you value your investment in Nicaragua, you'll do as I suggest."

"I hear you," Hartley said.

He slammed the door, but an instant later Cortez had slid over to the open window and was calling him. "Oh, Ronald," he said. "One other thing. Man to man." He was chuckling now. "I think you should realize that you've made your mark with Oriana."

"Oh?"

"Yes. I can tell by the way she talks to you. And believe me, Oriana wastes no time with people she doesn't like."

"It's good to have friends," Hartley said.

"Especially one like that, eh? I think she would be glad to see you again any time. So I hope you will seriously consider the possibility of a weekend with her on Mariposa. I'll be glad to provide whatever transportation you need." Cortez waved as the driver slipped the limousine into gear.

32

Hartley had to smile as Cortez's limousine pulled away from the curb. The *mordida* was in place, and there was no doubt what he had been offered in return for his political services: a trip to paradise with the best ass in Nicaragua. And as he walked beneath the Cruz de Cristo tree toward the hotel, he wondered how often Oriana had played this role for her protectors. Maybe at another time and in a more cynical mood, he might have been willing to accept the proposition as one of the perks of doing business, but on this day, after the events of the past twenty-four hours, he felt more angered by it than anything else. Sex and politics. And now they wanted him to become a political lobbyist! God Almighty! What was going on in the world? He wanted to protect the bank's investments, certainly, and maybe he should talk to Ambassador Grubbs, but the thought of encouraging support for the Guardia made his scalp tingle. And then, as he came up the two short steps to the portico, he saw the evening papers displayed in their racks beside the entrance, and he realized that talking to Grubbs would be totally unnecessary. The ambassador had already made up his mind, and it was no longer a small news item.

La Prensa was ablaze with the headlines: "U.S. Envoy Requests Military Aid." And reading the paper over a drink on the portico, Hartley felt both horrified and relieved to be let off the hook. According to the paper, the workers had returned to their jobs and business continued as usual in the city, but at Jinotega, the

Guardia had been hurt by the *Frente Sandanista Liberación Nacional*, or *FSLN*, as they were coming to be known, with their superior Russian Kalashnikovs and probable Cuban aid, and the ambassador felt that the time had come to strengthen the Guardia's arsenal with new U.S. weapons. Hartley finished his drink and sat for a moment. He thought he could see Karen's hand in the news release. It was smart, he thought, both the use of the press and the threat of new weaponry, politically and economically smart. But it all made him feel that he was caught defenseless in a kind of no man's land between opposing factions, and it troubled him enormously.

He drained his rum and orange juice and walked into the lobby, seeing nothing for a moment as he came out of the sunlight and waited by the bird cage as the macaw fluttered toward him rumbling with a voice like quietly rattling gravel, and then just as he was about to speak to the bird, he heard his own name called calmly from the back shadows of the room: "Ron...." And he turned to see Liliana curled on the corner of a sofa, small and dark and almost invisible to his sun-drenched eyes.

"Liliana?" His vision was clearing and he moved toward her, around the cage, pulling her to her feet and hugging her powerfully to his chest. "God! Let me look at you. I was afraid I'd never see you again...."

"I told you I'd be back."

"But what're you doing here? Where did you come from? Let me get my key."

He turned away and then turned back as though afraid to leave her. "God, it's so...."

She laughed and pushed him. "Go. Get your key."

In the elevator they did not speak, but once in the room, behind the locked door, he pulled her close, and she molded herself against him like sculptor's clay reshaping itself around his body. "You're unbelievable," he said. "So soft!" He kissed her lip, her cheek, her throat. "I was afraid," he whispered. "I thought you'd never come back."

"I told you—it was harder to stay away than I...."

"God, you're wonderful!"

He reached beneath her blouse and kissed her breast, and she closed her eyes, trembling slightly before she lifted his face with both her hands, pulling him up to look into his eyes. "We have to talk," she said.

"Talk? Now?" He ran his hands down her body.

"We have to...."

"It can wait."

"I told you I would never deceive you again."

"No, Liliana, please."

"I don't want you ever to think...."

But he kissed her mouth to silence and continued with her buttons, guiding her gently backward as their clothes fell away, cradling her tenderly, radiantly naked on the pillow, and pausing only to consume her for a moment with his eyes before moving down to kiss every part of her body, whispering her name, "Liliana..., Liliana..., Liliana...," as he entered her fully and the moment came when all control passed out of their hands.

For a long time afterward, they lay in total silence, clutching each other, skin to skin, as swimmers might clutch life preservers in troubled seas, drifting, dreaming, hearing far off the sounds of traffic and the five-noted song of the evening blackbirds that now were settling in the trees of the courtyard.

"I have been dead," Hartley said at last. She looked at him and kissed his cheek, and even in the fading light, he thought he could detect the glitter of teardrops in the corners of her eyes. "I have been dead, since the war, since my divorce, since Billy and...."

"Ron...."

"It's like coming back to life—like having another chance."

"Shhh...," Liliana said. "Shhh...," touching his face with her fingers. "Let me feel you a little longer, while the sun goes down."

It was nearly dark when they spoke again, and the floodlights were playing on the gilded facade of the theater and lighting all the battlements of the Palacio as Hartley went to close the curtains.

"Why don't we go find some food?" he said.

"We still have to talk."

"Whatever you want."

"No." She sat up, and her quiet composure seemed to vanish completely. "No. It can never be that way again."

"I don't understand."

"Whatever I want—don't you see? That's what I was afraid of. It can never just be *whatever I want*. There are two worlds," she said. "I live in two worlds now—the world with you and the other one. I wanted to keep them apart. I didn't come here for this."

He kissed her in the semidarkness, feeling suddenly helpless in the face of her agitation. "If you think I'm going to let you get away from me again, you're crazy."

"I swore there would be no love making. I needed you, but not as a lover."

"Are you sorry?"

"How can I be sorry? You made me very happy. For the moment, you made me very happy." She touched his hand. "But you made my life a million times harder."

"How can love make your life...?"

"Because now I'll be cautious. I didn't want to love anything but the idea of victory over Somoza, but now—oh God, I can already feel it coming—the thought creeping up the back of my mind that even if we don't win, there'll always be you, that there's Ron Hartley out there and he loves me and we can always have an O.K. life together somewhere else, and that makes me feel like a traitor."

"I've become the booby prize," Hartley said.

"No. Hardly. But you're an alternative. And part of me wants to protect that alternative with everything I've got. I'm more afraid now than...." She swallowed, and suddenly he saw the iron of resolution come back into the lines of her body as he had seen it once before. "I came to ask you a favor, Ronald. Up front. Not because you sleep with me. Not because you love me or I love you but—because I trust you, because I know you're competent, because I know you're humane. I wanted to *use* you, not love you. And now I've got it all muddled."

"Suppose I make it simple," Hartley said quietly. "Suppose I just refuse to do whatever it is you ask. Then we can go back to making love without all the strain."

She smiled very slightly, but disappointment was clear in her eyes. "You don't know what it is yet."

"Let me relieve you," he said. "I am not going to transport troops, and I am not going to carry arms or ammunition or any other illegal booty. So whatever else...."

"It's none of those," she said. "Not even one."

"Then...?"

"It's medicine."

"Medicine?"

"Yes."

"God! The one thing I didn't think of. Is it illegal?"

"Since when is saving life illegal?"

"You're a very clever woman," he said.

"No. Not clever at all."

"Yes."

"It's what I came for, Ron. A job that has to be done. It's why I tried to stop you—to stop us—to tell you before...."

"Very clever."

"I didn't want you to think I was using sex. I didn't! But I'm also a woman, and...." She pressed his hand to her cheek and kissed his fingers.

"It's hard to keep things from getting corrupted, isn't it?" Hartley said.

"Ron, as a friend, I ask you to fly this trip—call it a mercy mission, if you want to think of it that way. But as a lover, I don't ask you anything except to love me back."

"Will you still love me if I say no?"

"Ron...."

"Will you?"

She glanced down at the table and then back to look into his eyes. "Yes. But it'll be different," she said.

"How?"

"I won't see you much." She looked away toward the window.

"If you don't fly it, I have to find someone who will. I don't know where and I don't know who, and I don't know how I'll arrange to pay for it, but I'll do whatever is necessary. I'll be working with other men who believe what I believe."

"Let's go to dinner."

"Wait," she said. "Wait. We need to talk this out—now, before anything...."

"Look...."

She spoke suddenly louder than he had ever heard her: "Will you listen to me?"

"Yes. O.K."

"We have fourteen men who were wounded," she said. "They're going to die if we don't help." She whispered now, just inches from his face. "At least one has a gangrenous leg. Others are likely. They have no tetanus, no penicillin, no sulfa, no nothing unless it's alcohol from overproof rum. We've got supplies in San José, but that's five hundred miles across the jungle from Jinotega."

"I don't want to do it, Liliana. I'll be straight about it."

"These men will die."

"I know there's some other pilot who can do it."

"It's harder than you think. They all either work for the government or they have comfortable jobs with an airline and don't want to risk it—or they can't fly the planes we've got—or they want to charge a very high fee."

"Jesus!"

"But if you can take me, I can give the shots. Tetanus. Penicillin. Morphine to ease their pain and keep them out of shock. I learned all that when I was a stewardess. The rest...." She shrugged. "We do what we can."

"You don't realize what you're asking, Liliana."

"I'm asking you to help save lives!"

She put on her jacket, and for a moment as she stood alone at the window, Hartley felt that somehow now the whole bond between them had snapped like a tired rubber band. "I don't know how to act," she said. "If I'm affectionate, you'll think I'm trying to seduce you into going. If I stay away, you'll think I'm threatening to end it till I get my way."

"Isn't there some middle ground?"

"Oh, Ron...!"

He went to her and turned her face up to kiss her. "Why can't you get the pilot who flew you the last time—the one who flew you from here to San José?"

"Joel has five children. He doesn't want to take the risk. Besides, he's Costa Rican—not Nicaraguan. It's not his fight."

"It's not mine either, for God's sake!"

"Yes, but you've done it before."

"All the more reason not to do it again."

"These men will die!"

"And I'm sorry about that—really I am. But no—that's not enough. Joel doesn't want to take the risk. Well, neither do I. I can't think of any reason why any North American in his right mind should come down here and risk his skin to save a bunch of Nicaraguans who've been mutilating each other in endless civil wars since the country was founded."

"I suppose I'd better go," she said.

He watched her as she moved toward the bed to pick up her purse and he knew he'd gone too far. "I'm sorry," he said.

"Ron, it's hopeless. You're beginning to sound like all the other gringos who don't think we're quite human."

"I didn't mean it that way and you know it." She was at the door now. "Liliana, wait. Please stay."

"Ron...." She closed her eyes as though on the verge of a scream. "This is what I meant.... Oh, God help me! Two worlds! To live in one, I have to give up the other. I want to stay with you. Believe me. But if I stay—while we lie lovingly in each other's arms—men will be dying because, because—excuse me—because I wanted to fuck more than I wanted to get the medicine they need. I can't live with that. And if you won't do it, I have to find another way—now!"

She turned, almost running as she disappeared into the hall, refusing even to look back when he called her, and by the time he pulled on his shirt and got to the door, she was nowhere to be seen. He ran down the stairs, arriving in the lobby just as she pushed through the glass door and out toward the taxi stand, and for an instant, he thought quite consciously, "If you follow her, you're a fool." And then, as a cab driver held the door for her, he bolted forward, calling as he ran, "Liliana, wait!" He jerked open the cab door just as the driver started the motor. "Liliana, you didn't tell me everything."

"What?" She looked up blankly through the darkness.

"If we did it, would we fly back to the same field where we went before?"

"Un momento," she said to the driver. "Espéreme." She got out, pulling Hartley by his shirt toward the back of the car, speaking through clenched teeth, "Would you keep your voice down, *please*."

"Oh, I'm...."

"The answer is no. We would not fly to the same field. That's too dangerous now. There's another strip farther south. But that's one of the problems. It's only 2,000 feet long."

"God Almighty!"

"And trees at both ends. It takes a very good pilot."

"Is it paved?"

"No. Dirt. The miners made it, and then some drug traders—"

"The 411 will never get into that."

"But the 310 will," Liliana said. "We have to do it by daylight. In the morning. Before any afternoon rains come in."

"Liliana, I haven't flown a 310 in six, maybe seven years," Hartley said. "It's crazy. It's—"

"You're right," she said.

"What?"

"I said you're right. It's crazy. The more I think about it, the more I realize it. It's not your war, not your business, and I'm wrong asking you to get involved."

"But I am involved—involved with you."

"That's not a good enough reason and you know it." She turned back toward the waiting cab. "I'll smuggle it in another way."

He stopped her. "It'll be my last time," he said. "The very last time. If you'll accept that, then I'll do it. It'll be my chance to get back at the Guardia for that butt stroke against the side of my head, for killing those people in the street."

"O.K.," she said. She was smiling now. "O.K. I suppose those reasons are good enough."

"Now come back to the room."

"No, Ron. No. Don't you see? We've got to pick up the medicine in San José tonight."

33

It was easy then, once he'd made up his mind. "O.K." It was right, it was wrong, or maybe it had nothing to do with right and wrong at all. But suddenly it was his decision and he was completely sold to it. "O.K." He left her and sprinted back to the room for the charts she had brought him before. And then Liliana was soft beside him in the cab, pressing her bosom against his arm. "Thank you," she said. "You have made me a very happy woman."

"Tell me about it when we get back," he said. And the lights of the airport parking lot were glaring in front of them.

The left engine of the 310 was sluggish. First, it didn't want to fire at all, and then, after Hartley got it running, it didn't want to keep running. "I don't think it's flown since we brought it here," Liliana said.

"Has it been inspected?"

"I don't know."

"God! Flying these old planes may be the craziest thing of all." Hartley cut the switches and pulled all the documents he could find out of the glove compartment—license, air-worthiness certificate, work order for fuel filters.

"Fernando keeps all the logs in the office in San José."

"If we ever get to San José." He closed the compartment and went out again to inspect the engine, checking all connections with the flashlight. "Let's just wait," he said finally. "I've got it flooded now." In the darkness, he pulled the propeller through. "My guess is we've got some overtime spark plugs or maybe a faulty magneto."

But when he tried again, it caught, popping along unevenly for a few seconds as he coaxed it, until gradually it was firing on all cylinders and running almost smoothly. "There we go, baby, there we go," he said. "Now let's see if we can burn off a little of that carbon." He held the brakes and pushed the throttle to full forward, then leaned it out as far as it would go without stalling. When he finished, the left engine was running as smoothly as its mate on the right. "All other systems, except one radio, seem to work fine," he said. He looked at Liliana in the cockpit beside him. "O.K." he said finally. "We'll go. But I want a new set of plugs and maybe a new magneto in this plane before we leave San José."

From that point, everything went smoothly. When they pulled up to the PenAir hanger in San José, Liliana had two men to help load the cartons of medicine into the back of the plane, and by three A.M., she and Hartley were in her bedroom, wrapped again in each other's arms beneath a cotton blanket that shielded them from the mountain air. "This is the second craziest thing I have ever done," Hartley said.

"What was the first?"

"Going back to Vietnam."

"A second time?"

"It was a different assignment, but I felt like I had unfinished business there. So I went." He waited a minute in the darkness. "It cost me. My wife, my job, and, I think, my faith."

"Your faith?"

"In almost everything...."

"Maybe this time you can get some of it back."

"I'm open," he said. "But I remember a thing my mother used to quote: 'Blessed is he who hath no expectations, for he shall not be disappointed.'"

"That's awful!"

He laughed and pulled her closer in the darkness. "I certainly didn't expect *you*," he said. "And you feel wonderful! Like nothing else—like nobody I've ever known."

She kissed him and fitted her head beneath his chin. "I want you to know—right now," she said, "this moment may be the happiest moment of my life."

"How could that be, Liliana? How? Everything's so tentative."

"Maybe that's what makes it possible."

"You're amazing."

"Oh, I was happy in a way when I married Billy. But underneath it all was my parents' murder. Billy was escape for me. I was running away. But now, I'm not running anymore. I'm facing the danger and doing something about it."

"Wait."

"No. Listen. What I'm doing now is right and important and the man I love is helping me do it. And it's the happiest moment of my life. Simple as that."

"I wish I could see right and wrong as clearly as you do."

"You will, Ron. You will. I just know it."

There were no replacement spark plugs in stock at the airport. The mechanic was very apologetic. "We have them on order, Señor, but—"

"Then clean these," Hartley said.

"Ron, the time...," Liliana said.

He looked at her in her flight suit standing in the door of the hanger. "Do you know what kills pilots?" he said. "It's pretty women who urge them to take shortcuts."

"What if we get an early rain?"

"Then we'll go tomorrow."

"But—"

"Clean them," Hartley told the mechanic. "Gap 'em. Clean the mags, too. As soon as possible."

"Ron...."

"Those wounded men aren't going anywhere, Liliana," he said. "But this is your skin and mine. And getting out of a short field with a weak engine is no fun."

"I'll try to call Rubén."

"Good idea. See what the situation is."

But when she came back thirty minutes later, she was clearly worried. "Get your charts and computer and let's go inside," she said.

"What's the matter?"

"Come on." She led him into a room next to her cousin's office, and she was suddenly speaking almost in a whisper as she pointed to the map that Hartley spread on the table. "I couldn't get through to Rubén, but I talked to someone else. Most of the phone lines to Jinotega have been cut, and the Guardia has stepped up pressure all through the province. We need to change the route."

"We could go out to the Caribbean," he said. "Instead of over land, we could cut north above the San Juan River and go up the coast. Come in from sea side."

"O.K."

"But it's further. We'll be running on fumes."

"There's a field at the port of El Paisello," she said. "I don't know anything about it, but on the way back, we can stop if we have to."

By the time they walked back to the plane, the mechanic had the engines running, but he was not happy. "It is better, Señor, but you've got three weak plugs. I would like to change them all, if I had them."

"Yes."

"I matched them with good top plugs, and it is running fine now, but...." The little man shrugged.

"Right," Hartley said. "Thanks." He hesitated and looked at Liliana in the sunlight by the door of the plane.

"Ron, it's very late."

"It's crazy," he said. "Over jungle, ocean, God knows what...." He looked at her again, but she was totally undeterred, returning his gaze without the slightest hint of fear, somehow shaming him with the force of her determination. "Get in," he said. He shrugged and motioned toward the cockpit. "Not for anybody else," he said. "Understand that. Never would I do it for anybody else."

They buckled their seat belts as Hartley called ground control for clearance and moved out toward the end of the runway. "Is this an example of how you have no faith?" Liliana said.

"No," he said. He stopped for a final runup at the end of the taxiway, pushing the throttles forward to check the mags, and there was no way he could ignore the dip in RPMs as he switched from right to left. He checked them a second time. On "Both," they were normal. "No," he said again, "it has nothing to do with faith." And then he interrupted himself as he responded to the tower clearance, "PenAir 532 departing runway two-eight." He pulled onto the active and slipped the power forward to full, speaking loudly now above the engines as he felt the surge of thrust in the small of his back. "This is an example of *risk*, calculated risk, pure and simple." And by then the wheels had cleared the runway.

The trip out went smoothly. He curved up over the city, and once they were out of the mountains along the San Juan basin toward the coast, he dropped down to an altitude of about 500 feet, and soon they were skimming above the white-capped Caribbean surf. "Down here, we have just dropped out of everybody's radar screen," he said. "So far as the world knows, we have vanished into the ozone, and frankly, I don't think we should stop till we reach Miami."

She laid her open hand on his thigh. "First things first," she said. "We'll have the rest of our lives to go to Miami. Look, there's the port of El Paisello." She pointed across his left and lifted the folded map for him to see.

"O.K." he said. He could see four cargo ships at anchor in the harbor. "One of those ships probably has my tractors on it. Wanna go see?"

"No. Another time."

"O.K." He laughed and pulled farther out to sea to avoid the ships. "Then hand me that computer in your lap." He worked a quick calculation of ground speed. "One hundred forty miles north and then straight in ten miles on a heading of 270 degrees to the village of Flores and the field just south. If I'm right, we should hit it in about fifty-five minutes."

He was only three minutes late and that, he said, was because Flores was so little you couldn't tell whether you were seeing it or not. He circled it twice and then followed the river that curved southward almost invisibly beneath the overhanging vegetation until, on the right, boxed in by tall trees on three sides, he saw the unmistakable scar that was meant to serve as an airfield. "Jesus, help us!" was all he could say. "You want me to land on that!"

"It's all we've got."

"My God, it'll be a carrier landing! You need a helicopter."

"I told you it would be tricky."

"Tricky. Hell, Liliana, this will be only the second landing I've made in this type airplane in over seven years."

She shrugged. "If we had parachutes, we could drop the medicine and I would jump, but...."

"You're crazy, you know that?"

"Look who's flying me with a bad engine."

"Jesus!" He throttled back and dropped down to treetop level. "Let's go take a look."

There was a long corrugated building beside the runway and people now were standing outside to watch as he came down, buzzing just a yard above the strip before he pulled up at the far end. "The surface looks O.K." he said, "but what I wouldn't give now for an L-19 or a Beaver!" He climbed back to 500 feet and turned downwind. "O.K." he said. "You are about to see a standard, U.S. Army, fixed wing, vertical approach, executed by a rusty pilot in a plane that was never designed to do it. Your belt tight?"

"Yes."

He flipped on the auxiliary fuel pumps. "You say your prayers this morning?"

"Yes."

He started his landing checks aloud: "Gas. Undercarriage. Mixture. Props. Your will up to date?"

"Ron, will you stop!"

"No, I'm serious." He turned a short base leg and straightened out on final. "Flaps to full. You love me a lot?"

"Yes."

He raised the nose and pushed the throttle forward as the airspeed died. "Then pray that these engines don't cough for the next thirty seconds." He came over the trees hanging on the propellers, still with the nose high but descending sharply, hearing the stall warning scream through the cockpit and feeling the controls turn to mush as the airspeed bled away, knowing that if anything changed, either the wind or the power or the slightest degree of pitch, he could never salvage it. And then he was on the ground, hard on the main gear, bouncing twice and cutting the power as they rattled over the rough turf nearly to the trees at the far end before he braked it. "Jesus!" he said. Every fiber of his clothing was soaked. "You O.K.?"

"It was beautiful," Liliana said.

"A little rough."

"But gorgeous." She kissed his cheek as he turned the plane. "My bottom's sore."

"I'll massage it for you first chance I get." He pulled to a stop in front of the corrugated house. "I hate to cut the engines," he said. "Let's unload this stuff and get the hell out of here fast as we can."

"Ron, I've got to administer it. Change bandages. Dress wounds."

"Jesus!

"You can't just sit here burning gasoline in the hot sun."

He reached to kill the power. "Nothing's ever simple, is it?"

"Not here, no. You can help me, if you want."

"Go."

The people on the sidelines surged forward, chattering in their Spanish-Indian dialect as Liliana came out of the plane, and she— short as she was—seemed to tower over them, to be a mother to them, touching the women and the children, speaking as best she could, although she herself was having trouble with the dialect. "Did you bring food?"

"No. Only medicine."

"Clothing?"

"No. I'm sorry."

"Boots, shoes? We need shoes. The men are marching south through bad jungles."

"Just medicine. Help for the wounded, people who are sick."

And then Rubén Castillo came around the nose of the plane and embraced his sister as Tomás Rubio followed him into the sunlight, Rubio limping on his cane, now wearing fatigues and a pistol belt.

"Tomás!" Liliana said. Her arm was still around Castillo's waist. "I didn't know you'd be here."

"Yes, and we're grateful for what you're doing," Rubio said.

She embraced him, too, beside the wing. "Get the men to unload," she said. "We have—"

But Rubio was looking at Hartley stepping off the wing behind her, and his left hand went suddenly to his pistol. "Liliana, do you know who this man is?"

"Yes, of course."

"He's U.S.! A friend of people at the embassy!"

"Yes," Liliana said. "I know."

"How do you know he can be trusted?"

"I know him very well."

"He could be a spy."

"Ask him how he liked hiding from the Guardia in my hotel room," Hartley said.

"I've known him for years," Liliana said. "He has helped us. Now call the men and let's get started."

Hartley extended his hand, but Rubio merely looked into his eyes and turned abruptly to speak with the men who were waiting to unload the plane, and Hartley followed Liliana and Castillo into the building.

The smell of urine and sweat and decay met them like a stone barrier at the doorway, but they pushed on, and after an instant in the dim interior, they could see that the situation was much worse than anyone had suggested. Instead of fourteen wounded men and women, there were more than twenty people of all ages lying on pallets or on the bare floor. "God Almighty!" Hartley said.

But Liliana was already reaching to open the first carton of medicine. "Come on," she said. "There's a lot to do."

They broke the seal on the carton and began to arrange her supplies, but a moment later Rubio followed them in and touched Liliana's arm. "Wait," he said. "Before you start. Let me explain our situation. Time is everything." He led them into a corner with Castillo. "The Guardia has been pressing us," he said. "They are faster than we expected, but, except for the danger to our wounded, it is exactly what we wanted. While the Guardia is looking for us here at Jinotega, we are taking the main army south where we will meet another force to attack El Paisello."

"El Paisello!"

"Yes. We have supplies coming on a Panamanian ship, and now is the time for us to take the port. We think the United States...." He looked at Hartley. "I'm sorry, Señor, but we think the United States will resupply the Guardia and maybe even send troops. We want to act before that happens."

"Just a minute," Hartley said.

"No. Listen. The main attack force has already gone south. Castillo is leaving with the rear guard over land this afternoon. I will fly out with you and take as many wounded as we can."

"Wait," Hartley said. "Just hold it. I agreed to fly medicine—not bodies."

"Señor, it is absolutely necessary."

"No."

"Yes," Rubio said. "Absolutely necessary. I must coordinate the force at El Paisello. That man there...," he pointed to a pallet on the floor, "...you see him with the shattered leg, Jonathan Quetoda. He is our political organizer. He is in desperate need of a doctor. The man beside him near the wall is a demolition expert—Chavez. He has to train others in our new equipment. On the other side—"

"No!" Hartley said again. "I'm taking Liliana and maybe you but nobody else."

"I am in command here, Mr. Hartley."

"And I'm flying the airplane."

"Yes," Rubio said. "Of course." He reached into his pocket and held up the ignition key from the panel of the plane. "But only when I allow it."

"Jesus!" Hartley said. "Give me that."

"Only when we are on board."

Hartley stepped forward to grab the key, but Liliana was suddenly tugging at his arm as Rubio dropped his hand to the grip of his pistol. "Ron, come help me," she said.

"Liliana, look at him!"

"If we do not fly out together, Mr. Hartley, then we will not fly out at all," Rubio said.

Hartley pulled himself free and took another step, but by then Rubio's pistol was out of its holster.

"We're his prisoners, Liliana! Did you hear him?"

But Liliana was again tugging at his arm. "Come on, help me," she said again, and her voice was as calm as she could possibly make it as Rubio turned contemptuously away. "I'll talk to him. I know it's hard, but trust me. I'll talk to him and it'll be all right. But right now, I need you. We came to save lives, and I need you to help me."

He followed her then, still cursing under his breath at the trap he was in, but Liliana seemed totally unconcerned with his anger as she peeled back the lid of a carton and knelt beside a man who was twisted in pain from a bad stomach wound. "Not much we can do here," she said in English. "But we do what we can. Hand me the sterile needles."

He watched her technique and then, as the afternoon wore on, he started giving shots himself: tetanus, penicillin, morphine to two men with stomach wounds and to Quetoda, barely conscious, with his gangrenous leg. "Thank you," Quetoda whispered. "The pain is very bad."

"Yes, I know," Hartley said. "We'll do what we can." Quetoda's lips were dry and cracked, and Hartley held him upright for a swallow of water just before he drifted into unconsciousness from the effects of the morphine.

"I hope you'll take him," Liliana said. "Unless that leg comes off, he'll be dead in two days."

Hartley backed away, covering his face with the back of his arm from the smell of putrefaction, and then he heard it, the sound unmistakable through the hot afternoon, the distant snap of small arms fire followed by the heavy thudding "clumps" of mortar rounds dropping in rapid succession. "Wait a minute," he said.

"What?"

"Wait." He walked to the door, and the sound came again, this time with the added chatter of automatic weapons, and he moved quickly out and around the porch until he found Rubio in the shadow of the house with three other men looking at maps beside the plane. "Where are they?" he said. "Where's the firing?"

"Just west," Rubio said. "We've got a perimeter line until we get the wounded clear."

"Listen, we've got to get out now."

"Already?"

"It won't take but one bullet through a gas tank, through a tire—or through *me*—to queer your whole plan. I'll take Liliana and you."

"And Quetoda and Chavez and Zorillo?" Rubio said.

"No!"

"I'll have them brought out."

"No!" But Rubio would not stop, and Hartley ran past him into the building to where Liliana was leaning over a small girl with a shattered kneecap. "Come on," he said. "We're leaving and you've got to talk to Rubio."

"But we're not through."

"You've got to talk to Rubio. He's going to overload the plane if he can."

She stood and lifted the child in her arms. "Can we take her?" she said in English.

"Liliana, I'm trying to get rid of weight."

"She doesn't weigh half as much as the medicine we brought in."

Liliana turned and held out the child toward Rubio as he

came through the door. "We could put her in the baggage compartment."

"She is very pretty," Rubio said. "But I do not think she will kill many Guardia this week." He touched the child's cheek and turned abruptly away. "No. Put her down and come outside. If we have room for anything extra, we will take some of this medicine."

Liliana did not lay the child aside but carried her closely as they moved behind Rubio through the door and into the open where the sound of gunfire was closer, now coming in short sharp bursts from behind the wall of trees. At the plane, Hartley could see the men loading the last of three makeshift stretchers through the cargo door. "Tell him, Liliana," he said. "Tell him why it won't work."

She set the little girl beside the house and took Rubio forcefully by the arm, turning him to face Hartley. "You can tell him better," she said. "Go ahead."

"O.K." Hartley said. "Tomás, listen. It is a problem of weight, air density, and power. I would like to take everybody in that house. But the heavier the load, the longer it takes a plane to get off the ground. In hot, muggy weather like this, it's even worse. If you load the airplane with six people on this short runway, we will all end up in the trees at the other end. Dead! There's nothing I can do about it but refuse to fly it—which I will." He looked at Rubio's hand playing with the grip of his pistol. "And if you shoot me, it will only be a question of which end of the runway I die on."

"You are very hard, Señor."

"Physics is hard. In some areas, I know the difference between right and wrong very clearly, and this is one of them. No Zorillo and no Chavez." He pointed to the last two litters just loaded into the plane.

"Chavez has a lung wound," Liliana said. "He's in bad shape."

"Whose side are you on, for God's sake?"

Her eyes were suddenly very sad, but she did not speak as the sound of weapons fire came again and three more mortar shells dropped so close to the house that Hartley could feel the concussion against his skin.

"Now," he said. "It's time to move it now!"

"Take out Zorillo and Chavez," Rubio ordered. He handed Hartley the ignition key. "I cannot argue," he said. "Perhaps you could make a second trip...."

"One trip," Hartley said. He climbed into the plane and gagged at the smell of Quetoda's rotting leg in the close compartment. "Jesus!" he said. "Let's go. Get in." He opened the window for air and shouted, "Clear props on the right!" as he pulled the starter. The starboard engine turned and sprang to life, but when he looked back to start the left one, he found Liliana standing on the wing looking in at the window. "What the hell are you doing out there?" he said. "Get in!"

"Ron...."

But he was pulling the starter and the prop was turning as the engine ground over without catching, and he missed everything she said as he double-checked the switches and the throttle setting and engaged the starter again, grinding the engine through until it caught, first one cylinder and then another, popping reluctantly and then sending back a roaring cloud of black smoke as it finally responded and settled down. "Get in here," he yelled again, but he felt a movement in the cockpit beside him and turned to see Rubio sitting in the co-pilot's seat. "No," he shouted over the engines, "No, what're you doing here? Get out! Liliana!"

But Liliana was reaching through the open window to touch his face. "I'm not going," she said.

"The hell you're not! Get in here!"

"I haven't finished what I came to do."

"No! I won't go without you!"

"Chavez is in the back. Take him."

"No...!"

"If you make it back today, I'll go with you."

"Liliana...!"

"Otherwise, I'll walk out with Castillo."

"You're not equipped to walk a hundred miles through the jungle."

"Nobody is," she said, "but we'll do it. Now go!" Upwind, on the right side of the runway, three mortar shells dropped in—clump—clump—clump, sending up three geysers of smoke and stone and clay. "Go!" she shouted. "Now, before it's too late!"

She kissed her fingers and touched his face and jumped off the wing, not even looking back as she ran toward the waiting child. "Liliana!" Hartley thrust his head through the window, kneeling across Rubio's lap on the opposite side of the plane and shouting again as she disappeared into the house, "Liliana!" He reached toward the door to run after her, but just as he touched the handle another salvo of mortar rounds dropped in along the left side of the runway ahead, and he knew it would be only seconds before they would have it targeted. "God help us," he whispered. And he fell back into his seat and pushed the throttles forward, dropping flaps as he taxied to the takeoff end and turned to add full power.

"God help us," he said again. And then they were flashing down the runway with the nose wheel slightly raised and an airspeed already touching seventy as they came abreast of the house and heard the shells clumping in again, and from the corner of his eye he could see the house disintegrating in flame and smoke and sending fragments hurtling across his canopy, and "Oh Jesus!" was all he could say.

He forced himself not to look back. His airspeed had reached seventy-five by then, but he held it on the ground to reach eighty before he racked back on the yoke, and the plane leapt almost vertically upward with the disappearing gear barely touching the tiny branches as they cleared the trees.

He was soaked with sweat, and suddenly he wanted to vomit. But he held it, swallowing hard and opening the window again to clear the cabin of the smell of Quetoda's dying leg as he turned back now to parallel the runway, not able to leave until he'd seen the worst and whispering again and again, "Oh, Jesus, Jesus, Jesus," as he looked below at the burning house and the bodies strewn like debris across the yard and the attacking Guardia soldiers running to fire their rifles at the plane as he turned outward toward the sea.

They did not speak. All the way to El Paisello, Hartley and

Rubio, riding side by side, five hundred feet above the jungle and down the coast 120 miles to El Paisello, they did not speak. Once, as Hartley banked to pick up his southern compass heading, he glanced into Rubio's eyes, but neither man had words for what had just happened, and after that, they did not even make eye contact until, on the ground in El Paisello, they opened up the back of the plane and found Chavez lying in a pool of blood. "Oh my God!" Rubio said then. But Hartley just stood back and stared as Rubio's two Indian helpers lifted out the body. Four Guardia bullets had stitched a line of holes across the mid-section of the plane, and one of them had shattered Chavez's spine.

"What a disaster!" Rubio said to Hartley then, "what a disaster! No one knew demolition like Chavez. Your navy trained him." He reached across the body and removed the pistol from Chavez's belt.

"Looks like we lost it all, this trip," Hartley said.

"I hope we can justify it," Rubio said. And for the first time his eyes showed sadness without contempt. "At least we've got Quetoda. He is so very good making people understand our revolution."

The two Indian men had lifted Quetoda's unconscious body into the waiting van and now suddenly were standing beside Rubio in the darkness. "Ready, Gaspar?"

"Yes," Gaspar said. "I know a doctor who will help."

"I need gasoline," Hartley said.

"See the man over there." Rubio pointed to a small building beside the runway. "I don't think you'll have trouble. Many strange things are unloaded at El Paisello." He extended his hand. "Good luck."

And then, as Rubio and the others drove away in the van, Hartley closed his eyes and leaned his cheek against the smooth aluminum skin of the plane. His mouth had the taste of brass, and he knew that his nostrils would never be clear of the smell of Quetoda's leg, and for a moment all he could see was smoke and fire and fragments flying past his canopy as the house went up, and his knees nearly buckled beneath him. Could she have lived? he wondered, and if she survived the blast, could she survive capture by the Guardia? Probably not, and probably she would not want to, and he hoped it had been quick, that she had gone without pain before the attacking soldiers found her. But—and suddenly, as the picture of the exploding house washed over him again, he found himself praying that somehow it was not so, that somehow she had not stopped in the house. He knew the odds, 99 to 1, worse. But there beside the plane, he closed his eyes until lightning flashed inside his lids, praying with all his heart that somehow she had continued running straight through the house to join Castillo in the jungle, praying against all reason that somewhere in the darkness, she rested now beneath the trees with the broken child in her arms.

34

Hartley flew into Managua without lights. It was dangerous, he knew, risky and illegal in every country in the world. But he was, he realized, a fugitive, the pilot of a bullet-riddled, stolen airplane that was covered with blood. And the danger of flying dark and unannounced into a controlled airfield seemed as nothing compared to the danger of being captured by anybody's police force. If the Israelis could do it at Entebbe, he could do it at Managua, he thought.

So he killed his running lights and monitored Managua Approach Control as he came across the city, slipping in just above the housetops, and rotating his head like a beacon to scan for other aircraft until he found the active runway and saw the way was clear to bring it in quickly behind a departing Eastern Airlines flight to Miami.

He touched down right at the green line and braked fast to pull off the concrete onto the grass, where he shut it down and scrambled into the darkness across the little blue lights of the taxiway and over the fence at the boundary of the field. For a while, he stayed quietly in the bushes, but when it seemed that no major alarms had been set off, he made his way to the terminal and found a taxi that could take him into town.

"I am ill," he told the hotel clerk when he arrived. And he closed himself away, dumping the fistful of waiting messages on the table and sitting on the bed with the telephone to dial first the U.S. Embassy, where he got only a recorded message about hours, and then to dial Karen, where he got no answer at all. And then, still sitting up and fully clothed, he fell into repeated waking dreams of fire and explosion and airplanes that would not fly and Liliana calling for him and Liliana bleeding out her life beside the runway until he knew he must have fallen asleep because the sunlight was shining in his face and the telephone was ringing in his hand and the air around him was filled with the familiar combat smell of his own sweat and fear. He answered and heard Brad's voice sounding distant and confused at first but then coming through loudly above the echo of satellite transmission: "Ronnie? God damn! Where have you been?!"

There was no way he could explain and be understood. "I've been sick, Brad."

"Sick?"

"Yes."

"Are you all right now?"

"Yeah. I think so."

"I've been trying to call you for two days."

"I'm sorry."

"Walter Guy at Ajax Equipment says he can't reach anybody in Nicaragua to check on the tractors."

"Things have been confused," Hartley said.

"The news sounds like we've hit the middle of a war. The president just sent a new shipment of arms down there."

"I haven't heard any news today."

And suddenly Brad was almost shouting with frustration. "Ronnie, what're you doing?"

"I told you I've been sick."

"Did you see a doctor?"

"No. But I'm O.K. now."

"Just how bad is it?" For a moment, he thought Brad was inquiring about his health, but Brad's next question corrected his mistake. "Is our investment in danger?"

"I think..., they'll be able to contain it. I can tell you more by tomorrow."

"Damn it, Ronnie, we sent you down there to stay on top of

things."

"I'm sorry, Brad. I told you...."

"Do you need to come home?"

"No. That is, I don't know. I'll call you tomorrow."

"Ronnie, remember. We insured that equipment ourselves. It's ours till it's in their hands. Pull whatever strings you have to, but stay with it till they take possession."

For a long moment, Hartley was totally silent.

"Ron, are you there?"

"Yeah, Brad. I'm here."

"What the hell's going on with you?"

"I'm thinking, Brad, thinking what I have to do." But even as he spoke, other words were filling his throat like a goiter. He didn't want to talk to Brad and he didn't want to pursue the fate of any piece of equipment for Agri-21. He wanted out. "Oh, Jesus!" he wanted to shout into the telephone. "Brad, I quit! I resign forever. I want out of finance, out of industry; I want out of politics, out of business, and out of military operations of any kind whatsoever!" But instead of saying any of that, he simply repeated himself. "I'll check on it and call you tomorrow."

And then as he hung up exhausted and fell back on the bed, his eyes were filled with tears. Suddenly all he could see was Liliana, Liliana touching the women as she came out of the plane, Liliana bandaging the wounded, Liliana with the crippled child in her arms, Liliana who had dared him to choose sides in a conflict that he knew now was not just the conflict in Nicaragua but the conflict of every country in the world—the desire for wealth and privilege versus the desire to maintain human rights and feed the poor— and then Rubio with his hand on the grip of his pistol: "If we do not fly out together, Mr. Hartley, we will not fly out at all." And anger washed over him like a fever.

He had wanted to kill Rubio, and yet he had flown him to safety. Was it cowardice? he wondered. Had it been the simple desire to save his own ass that had made him stay that extra minute in the cockpit instead of throwing Rubio off the plane and forcing Liliana to ride out with him? Losses, all losses, he thought. And what would have been the use? Even if he had overpowered them both and strapped Liliana to the seat without getting shot, what would have been the use if they had then been blown to mincemeat on the runway thirty seconds later? Losses, all losses. Even for the survivors. We make our choices. We live or die with the results.

And then, in what seemed no more than an instant, the telephone was again ringing loudly beside the bed, shocking him through the silence of the room, and again he let it ring twice more before he answered and heard the dark voice of Daniél Cortez. "Ah, Mr. Hartley, if I had known you were ill, I would have sent my personal physician," he said when Hartley told him of being sick.

"That's very kind," Hartley said.

"I tried to call earlier to let you know that our tractors and equipment are in the harbor at El Paisello, but we haven't been able to unload the ships because of the strike."

"I see," Hartley said. "When?"

"We're going to take our own men and do it tomorrow. Would you like to go with me to receive them?"

Hartley hesitated, counting, one day, two, three, wondering now how long it would take Castillo's force to make the march from Jinotega to link up with Rubio's force in El Paisello.

"Mr. Hartley?"

"Sorry. I was thinking." He waited another moment. "Have you heard of any rebel movement in that area? Any threat to the port?"

"No," Cortez said. "Of course, rebels appear in strange places, but we think we have broken their force. After the promise of U.S. aid, the rebels seemed to dissolve. Jinotega has proved to be a great victory for us, after all."

"Where is Colonel Negroponte?"

"In Jinotega. Why do you ask?"

"Will he be back before the tractors are unloaded?"

"No. I doubt it. We want to put the heavy equipment on trucks tomorrow. The tractors can be driven from the port, all in a convoy the day after."

"With military escort?"

"Some, yes. Why?"

"I don't want to be caught in a cross fire. Hold on."

Hartley stood then, trailing the telephone line as he moved away from the stale bed. The tractors would be sitting ducks, he thought. If even half of Castillo's force made it to El Paisello, the tractors wouldn't stand a chance in convoy over the poor roads. And could Liliana be among the rebels? He stepped further away from the bed, standing now in the center of the room. In any world of reality, he knew there wasn't a chance, and yet.... "I haven't forgotten you," he said to Cortez. "I'm still here. I'm trying to check my schedule."

The tractors. He could protect them, he thought. And one tip to the Guardia was all it would take.

And then he almost shouted at himself, "No!" It was insane. No. Not for tractors, not for money, not for anything he could name. He wanted to shout it, "No!" But he only breathed deeply and lifted the phone again, breathing carefully to control his anger at himself, "I'm sorry," he said. "I won't be able to go. I have another appointment, but I would like to see the equipment when you get back."

"All right," Cortez said. "I'll call you."

"Have a good trip," Hartley said.

And then, after a full minute without moving in the silent room, Hartley picked up the phone again and dialed. He waited through four rings and began speaking without preliminaries when Karen answered at the embassy, "I want to report a *missing* U.S. citizen," he said.

"What? Ron?"

"Yes."

"Who? Who's missing?"

"Liliana Castillo Summerfield."

"Where?"

"At Jinotega."

"God! You don't make it easy, do you? How do you know?"

"She was my best friend's wife," he said. And then he began to invent, "Her family asked me to find her, to see that she's O.K.—or else to take her body home for burial, in Virginia."

"I didn't know we had any Americans in that area at all."

"She went to take medicine to relatives and got caught. They think she's wounded."

"Can you identify her?"

"Yes, of course. Just get me clearance with the military. I'll go to Jinotega, wherever's necessary...."

"You'll have to come to the embassy."

"Put me in touch with the chief of staff, Colonel Negroponte."

"Rick usually takes care of that sort of thing, and he's not here."

"When will he be back?"

"I don't know."

"Karen, we can't wait!"

"Ron—"

"We have to move now."

"You'll probably have to work through Segura."

"God!"

"Rick knows the procedure."

"Will you call Segura?" He could hear her sudden intake of breath, and it seemed as though he could almost hear the wheels turning in her head before she spoke again. "Karen?"

"Ron..., it's difficult."

"Difficult, hell! We just gave his government weapons, for God's sake. They've endangered an American. Will you call him, or shall I go straight to the ambassador?"

"Yes. All right. I'll call him."

"O.K."

"I'll, I'll do it right away."

"O.K.," Hartley said again. "Do whatever it takes." He breathed deeply, then moved across the room, now moving quickly, crossing the space in two quick steps to hang up the phone. "I'm on my way to the embassy," he said. "We've got to move as fast as possible."